PRAISE FOR

Book of Dreams

"Inventive and incisive, Bunn's fiction never disappoints. And he's scored again with *Book of Dreams*. Don't miss this one."

—Jerry B. Jenkins, *New York Times* bestselling author of
the Left Behind series

"*Book of Dreams* is wonderful. Davis Bunn has created a literary delight that underscores the power of God's word. A page-turner with an inspiring supernatural element. I could not put this down."

—Anne Graham Lotz, bestselling author of *Just Give Me Jesus*

"*Book of Dreams* is an exceptional story. The concept itself is re-markably fresh, with a genuinely unique design. There are very few inspirational-style concepts that have the potential to cross over and become major mainstream hits. In my opinion, *Book of Dreams* is at the top of this list. Exciting, relevant, and accessible. A remarkable story, one that will linger long after the book is put down."

—Norman Stone, producer/director of *Shadowlands*

"*Book of Dreams* is a fascinating read. A totally new concept, which makes it a rare achievement. The story really makes you think. The theme is both very challenging and mesmerizing. A first-rate effort."

—Hy Smith, former executive vice president
of United International Pictures

HIDDEN

in

DREAMS

HIDDEN

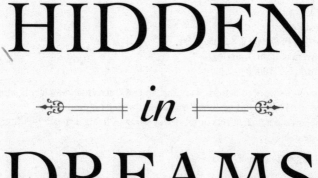

in

DREAMS

A Novel

DAVIS BUNN

HOWARD BOOKS
A DIVISION OF SIMON & SCHUSTER, INC.

NEW YORK   NASHVILLE   LONDON   TORONTO   SYDNEY   NEW DELHI

Howard Books
A Division of Simon & Schuster, Inc.
1230 Avenue of the Americas
New York, NY 10020

First Howard Books trade paperback edition July 2012

HOWARD and colophon are trademarks of Simon & Schuster, Inc.
For information about special discounts for bulk purchases,
please contact Simon & Schuster Special Sales at 1-866-506-1949
or business@simonandschuster.com.

The Simon & Schuster Speakers Bureau can bring authors to your live event. For
more information or to book an event contact the Simon & Schuster Speakers
Bureau at 1-866-248-3049 or visit our website at www.simonspeakers.com.

Designed by Jaime Putorti

Manufactured in the United States of America

10 9 8 7 6 5 4 3 2 1

Library of Congress Cataloging-in-Publication Data
Bunn, T. Davis
Hidden in dreams : a novel / Davis Bunn.
p. cm.
1. Dreams—Fiction. 2. Psychological fiction. I. Title.
PS3552.U4718H55 2012
813'. 54—dc23
2011047798

ISBN 978-1-4165-5672-5
ISBN 978-1-4516-6381-5 (ebook)

HIDDEN

in

DREAMS

1

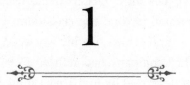

Elena dreaded the end of class.

She had already identified the students who were poised to attack. There were three of them, clustered at the front right corner of the room. Faces shining with anticipation.

They might as well be sharpening knives.

As soon as class ended, they leapt forward. But it was not three students. It was five. And Elena had no chance of escape.

"Dr. Burroughs, will you sign my book?"

Some of the other students clearly had no idea what all the fuss was about. Out of the corner of her eye she saw them hovering at the back of the classroom by the door, watching and talking among themselves.

Wanting to get it over with, Elena autographed the books, responded to the students' eager questions, and ushered them out; she hardly heard her own words. After shutting the door on their excited chatter, Elena walked to the window and stared at the rain. There was no reason this classroom should feel like a prison with plate-glass bars.

She had, after all, received exactly what she had asked for.

The previous year had basically been a disaster. Elena considered herself an optimist by nature, tempered by a hefty dose of realism. But she had no trouble with the truth, even when it bent and twisted her most recent memories into a torrent as steady as the rainfall beyond the classroom window. Her year had started badly and grown steadily worse. At the end of January, the insurance company had refused to pay for her home, which had been destroyed by fire. They claimed there was some doubt over whether she had had a hand in starting the blaze. The resulting court case looked certain to drag on for several years. Her lawyers were confident, but this did not fill the hole in her bank balance.

In February, the Oxford clinic where she had practiced decided not to reinstate her. Too much bad publicity related to her leave of absence, they claimed. The director had actually said her career was fatally tainted.

In March, the romance she had hoped to start with Antonio, her Italian financier, fizzled out. There was no acrimony. The spark simply died, and they both knew it.

In April, Lawrence Harwood, the other mainstay of her international prayer group, suffered a mild heart attack. At the insistence of his wife, Lawrence retired from the US financial oversight committee. His replacement had no interest in being connected to Elena. Just like that, the group she had sacrificed so much to help found disbanded.

Which led to May, June, and July. And the multiple whirlwinds that had landed her here.

Reluctantly, Elena had spent much of the spring revising *Book of Dreams* to bring the six-year-old text up to date. Her publisher begged Elena to do another publicity tour. Though she loathed the idea, Elena was desperate both for money and something to fill the empty days.

Her summer had been simply awful. Three months of airports and hotels and television appearances and lecture halls. She traveled and spoke and lived in a state of perpetual jet lag. Her prayers had become a simple litany, often spoken from the backseat of another taxi.

Then at an Atlanta appearance, the president of Atlantic Christian University approached Elena and offered her a chair, which was the academic name for a professorship that had been funded by an outsider. ACU had received a substantial grant from an alumnus to help build its psychology department and were looking for a name. Elena would teach several classes but have ample time to write or continue with her private practice. The president described the city of Melbourne as a quiet haven nestled between Cape Canaveral and the glitz of south Florida. Elena had almost wept with gratitude, and called the offer an answer to a prayer.

Now, she was not so sure. Especially since the local forecasters talked about a hurricane bearing down on their coast, as though the weather was determined to show her just how bad things could become.

"Dr. Burroughs?"

Elena turned from the window and felt her heart stop. There in the doorway stood Miriam, her best and oldest friend.

The problem was, Miriam had died the previous summer.

The woman stepped into the empty classroom and closed the door behind her. "I'm Rachel Lamprey. Perhaps you remember me?"

Elena felt her chest unlock. The woman's resemblance to her late sister was astonishing. "Of course. We met at Miriam's funeral."

"I know I should have called. But I was afraid you wouldn't see me."

Rachel Lamprey was impossibly elegant. It was not merely her designer outfit of rough silk, shaded like ancient bone china. Nor was it the perfect coiffure, the heels, the pearls, or the small Cartier watch. Rachel Lamprey held herself with a queenly elegance. As though she expected the world to do her bidding. And do so because she deserved it.

Miriam had seldom spoken of her younger sister, or the rift that had kept them apart. Elena recalled how once Miriam had mentioned her sister's casual ruthlessness. Miriam had called it a throwback to some distant era, when their forebears had held the power of life or death over thousands. Another time, Miriam had mentioned Rachel's disdain toward faith. Rachel considered herself too intelligent and too modern to need any God, Miriam had said. Standing before the haughty woman, Elena decided that other than the physical resemblance, Rachel possessed none of Miriam's most vital qualities. "Won't you sit down?"

"Thank you, no. I have something of vital importance to discuss and very little time. Could we perhaps find somewhere more private?"

Elena was not certain she wanted to go anywhere with this coldly aloof woman. "Is this about your daughter?"

"Penelope?" She sniffed. "Hardly. Whatever gave you that idea?"

"You two argued through Miriam's funeral. I thought, well, with my clinical background—"

"My daughter has spent her entire life indulging in phases, Dr. Burroughs. When we were in London for Miriam's service, Penny was consumed by gothic rock. I ordered her to leave her black garbs and body piercings at home. Penny was not pleased. We argued. Now she is obsessed with whales. Penny uses such phases as an excuse to redesign her entire personality, wardrobe, lifestyle. She becomes enraged and sullen when the world refuses to go along with her latest fad. Unfortunately my daughter has no idea who she truly is. No one does."

"Perhaps these phases are your daughter's lonely cry to be loved and accepted by her mother," Elena replied sharply. "Only she has grown so accustomed to your disdain she has either forgotten or repressed the original longings. She enters into each new phase expecting to fail in your eyes."

"You sound just like Miriam."

"I consider that the finest compliment I've received in a very long while."

"Another point on which we must disagree." Rachel Lamprey glanced at her watch. "I am expected at a board meeting in Orlando at four. Could we perhaps step into your office?"

"Sorry, no. It is full of boxes."

"Oh, very well." She walked over and opened the door. Instantly a wash of student noise filled the room. She spoke to someone unseen. A young man followed her back inside. "This is Reginald Pierce. My deputy."

"Dr. Burroughs." The young man was dressed in a pinstriped shirt, suspenders, gold cuff links, dark tie. He moved like a dancer. Or a fighter. Elena could not be certain which. His movements were as smooth as they were swift. He extracted a small device from his briefcase, extended the antennae, and swept the room. "You're clean, Ms. Lamprey."

"See we're not disturbed."

"You have ten minutes. Otherwise—"

"I'm well aware of the time issue." She stepped to the windows and pulled down one shade after another as Reginald left the room.

"What are you doing?"

"It's possible for an observer to bounce a signal off plate glass, turning any window into a listening device. Your shades will render this impossible. It's unlikely that anyone was able to track us. Reginald is very thorough. But we can never be too certain."

The room was bathed in a vague gloom. Elena seated herself slowly behind her desk. This woman clearly was comfortable only when in utter control. "Won't you have a seat?"

Instead, Rachel Lamprey began pacing in front of Elena's desk. "I am trained as a biochemist. Perhaps Miriam told you that. I am well aware of how my sister pushed you into sharing her obsession over dreams. I positively detested Miriam's determination to taint every discussion and every topic with her religious obsession."

Elena's chair creaked as she shifted. "Two points of clarification. Miriam was not obsessed. And the issue was not religion, but faith."

"Another point on which we must disagree." Yet Rachel Lamprey showed no irritation. At least, not at Elena. "My division at SuenaMed, my company, is at the point of making a major breakthrough. The news will be announced at any moment. And yet here I am, forced to take time I do not have, to deal with an issue related to dreams."

Elena found herself resuming her mode as a clinical analyst. Listening and watching and absorbing. It was as if she had slipped into an old favorite suit left at the back of her closet for far too long. Elena could thus separate Rachel Lamprey from the memory of her sister. Because whatever else Rachel might be, she was most certainly not Miriam.

Rachel's heels formed a sharp cadence across the linoleum tiles. "Dreams and foretelling have been a burden or a calling or a passion or an obsession that has remained with my family for centuries. I call it by different names depending upon the season."

Elena asked, "How do you refer to it now?"

Rachel's glittering black eyes held a fierce intensity. "I have no idea."

"What has changed?"

"My division is confronting an issue that specifically relates to your work on dreams." Rachel faced her squarely. "One of my clinical patients has been having dreams that follow a very disturbing pattern. The sequence is precise. Repetitive. And overwhelming in its power."

"I don't understand. You fear this is due to some adverse reaction to your new drug?"

"I did. At first." Rachel Lamprey's eyes flashed a dark fire. "Until I learned that others with no discernible connection to our company were having the same dream."

2

Reginald Pierce must have been listening at the classroom door, because he opened it the instant Rachel started down the center aisle.

She demanded, "You have the flash drive?"

"Of course."

"Leave it with Dr. Burroughs."

Reginald stepped into the classroom. "The chairman called."

Rachel blanched. "When?"

"Five minutes ago. I said you'd be coming out of the conference soon. You are to phone him immediately."

"I'll be in the car." She started to leave, then paused. "Forgive me, Dr. Burroughs. This day is fraught. And our chairman . . . Look through the material and call me, would you please. And soon. Please. Good-bye."

Reginald set his alligator attaché case on Elena's desk and popped the locks. "Can you help her?"

"That's an interesting way to phrase your question," Elena replied. "She does not need help often, does she?"

Up close, Reginald possessed a spicy scent, like the fragrance of some uninhabited Caribbean isle. He was strikingly hand-some, in a preppy and tightly wound sort of way. "Personally, I can't get my head around this dream stuff. But it has Rachel seri-ously rattled."

"You genuinely care about her," Elena observed.

He held out a memory stick. "Nothing rattles Rachel Lam-prey."

Elena accepted the stick. She felt the young man's fingers trembling, or perhaps the memory stick held a force so potent it created a vibration all on its own. "I see."

He gave her a business card. "My own details are on the back. You can contact me day or night." Reginald shut the case and started for the door. "She wasn't kidding. You really do need to hurry. You know. Just in case she's right. And this really is a crisis in the making."

When she returned to her rented condo, Elena turned on her tablet computer and popped in the memory stick. Her fourth-floor balcony overlooked the southernmost portion of the Banana River. Farther north, the river was over three miles wide and separated from the inland waterway by Merritt Island, a peninsula jutting south from Cape Canaveral. From Elena's balcony she could see the narrow spit where Merritt Island ended, marked by a drawbridge much loved by locals and tourists alike. Here the Banana River was crimped down to just fifty meters wide. It was quiet here, on the western side of the barrier island. The tourists clustered over by the Atlan-tic Ocean, where the hotels and the beachfront condos rose like concrete teeth. The traffic was heavy there, and the glitz was as constant as the noise. Over here it was still possible to savor the fragrances of frangipani and bougainvillea and old Florida.

Her apartment complex was a cluster of four low-slung buildings fronted by palm trees and docks for pleasure craft. The boat traffic was held strictly to a crawl, because the manatees used the narrow water as a haven for birthing their young. As Elena sipped her iced tea, a pod of river dolphins passed. She could hear the soft puff of their breaths as the westering sun turned their backs into slick copper. It was as good a place as any to call home.

Elena set down her drink and turned her attention to the tablet.

When she had completed her first read-through of Rachel's documents, Elena entered the condo and made a Cobb salad for dinner. She stood up to eat, watching the golden glow of another Florida sunset. The afternoon storms had passed, leaving the skies amazingly clear. The air remained very humid, the temperatures in the low nineties. Elena found she minded neither. Her screened balcony had a ceiling fan, which shifted the air enough to dry her perspiration almost as soon as it formed. She loved padding around in a sleeveless T-shirt and cotton shorts. Formal attire around here meant a shirt with a collar. She found it positively refreshing after Oxford's stuffiness.

When the salad was eaten, she returned to the chair and the tablet. Rachel's information came in two segments. The first was a file of clinical data, supplying an overview of SuenaMed's new drug. The medicine was a new means of treating ADHD in both children and adults. If successful, it could revolutionize the entire field of attention disorders. Elena could only imagine the pressure Rachel Lamprey was facing as the company approached its worldwide release date.

The second file contained a video named simply, "Clinical Debriefing, Patient 303." The file was dated two afternoons ago. Elena hesitated, then clicked on the tab.

The setting was a well-appointed office. The camera was situated so that it looked across the desk and focused on the chair and its occupant. The desk appeared to be black lacquer. A sterling silver clock read the same time as the file's heading. A vase held a spray of orchids.

Elena heard Rachel's voice say, "Will you describe the experience for me, please?"

"I already told the lab guy everything."

"I understand. And I've read his report. Which is why I asked to see you." Rachel's tone was soothing. She offered her guest a genuine concern. Despite Elena's doubts about the woman, she found herself impressed with Rachel's professionalism. "I'm very grateful for your taking the time to see me. A personal discussion is called for, given the details you gave my lab technician. Wouldn't you agree?"

The man appeared extremely nervous. He was overweight, almost round, and showed a clinical disconnect from his personal appearance. It could have been caused by his agitated state, but Elena did not think so. He wore a blue and yellow and green short-sleeved shirt, a web belt, and creased khaki trousers. His hair, though short, was unruly, as though he had not brushed it in days. Elena knew such traits were common in severe adult ADHD cases.

The patient asked, "Am I having these dreams on account of your spray? 'Cause if I am, I want out. Today."

"There have been over three hundred patients in our human trials," Rachel replied calmly. "These trials have now entered the third phase and have been going on for almost two years. No one, I repeat, not a single other individual, has reported anything like your symptoms."

The man was distraught. "So what am I supposed to do?"

"Before we discuss treatment, I would be grateful if you would please describe your symptoms for me."

"What are you, some kind of doctor?"

"I am a clinical biochemist. I am also director of this project."

Elena had the distinct impression the man was unaware of being videotaped. Which was not entirely ethical, since most clinicians would make an official statement with each new taping. The patient had undoubtedly signed release forms before beginning the trial. Which would legally cover this. But Elena disliked the secretive corporate nature revealed in this action.

Rachel pressed gently, "You have been involved in this study for how long?"

"I got my first spray last week. Today was supposed to be dose two. Now I ain't so sure."

"And the dreams began immediately after the first dose?"

"Nah, it was three nights ago. But it ain't no dream. It's an attack."

"Who attacks you, sir?"

"The thing, the place, all of it. Over and over."

"So the dream is repetitive."

"Nine, ten times now. It comes more than once every night."

"Will you describe it for me, please?"

Elena gripped the tablet with both hands. When the patient leaned forward, she did the same. Caught up in the man's evident fear. And everything that had come before in her own life.

"It starts out, I'm standing in the bank lobby. The line, it just goes on forever. Out the doors and down the block and back for miles. I'm in line but I see this too. Don't ask me how. I've been standing there for, like, days. We all have. And we're scared."

"You share this sensation of palpable fear with the others standing in line?"

"All of us. Every last one. You bet."

"What precisely are you afraid of?"

"I don't know. Not then."

"What happens next?"

"The line starts moving. Only the fear, it just gets worse. I'm so scared, man." Dark patches streaked the patient's shirt. His face glistened. His voice shook as he continued, "Finally it's my turn. I tell the lady behind the counter, I want all of it. Every dime. It's mine and I want it now.

"She goes, 'Certainly, sir.' And she dumps this load of confetti on the counter. I can see it's money. But it's been shredded. Worthless. Then I wake up."

"Can you describe for me the moment of waking?"

He wiped his face with both hands. "I'm screaming my head off."

"I understand this is very difficult for you. I genuinely appreciate the effort this requires."

The patient's haunted expression said he knew what was coming.

Rachel asked, "Is there anything more you would like to share with me?"

The patient mashed his hair down tight to his skull. Over and over.

"Any lingering impression or feeling that might—"

"I got to tell somebody."

"Excuse me?"

"You asked what I feel. That's it. That's why I'm sitting here. Going through this again. Because I got to. You hear what I'm saying?"

"You are telling me that you are filled with a strong urge to share this dream."

"I already told you, lady. This ain't no dream."

"What would you prefer that I call it, then? What word would you say best—"

"A warning."

"Is this warning intended for you?"

"For everybody. That's what I feel. It's either stand on the street corner and shout, or sit here and tell you. I figure, if I'm nuts, this is at least a way to keep it private."

Rachel did not speak.

"Am I nuts?"

"Nothing you have expressed to me indicates any abnormal symptoms," she replied slowly. "Other than your evident stress."

His laugh was coppery with weakness. "You got that right."

The screen went blank.

3

Elena arrived in the president's office at eight the next morning. She had woken in the middle of the night with a desperate need to speak with someone she trusted. The problem was, she knew almost no one in the entire state of Florida.

The Atlantic Christian University campus was divided into two distinct components. The original low-slung buildings dated from the early seventies, when the university had been founded. Florida tended to age buildings with a harsh hand. Years could pass with little more than summer thunderstorms and lightning strikes. Then a hurricane could roar through. Locals said a hurricane aged a building ten years in one week. The past six years had been kind to the Space Coast, as this region was known. But in 2003 the coast had been hit by two category-three storms in the space of seventeen days. The following year, a storm landed on the opposite coast as a category one, then somehow managed to gather force as it crossed the state. It tore into Melbourne from the west, from the landward side, and then sat over the region for nineteen hours, spawning twenty-seven tornados and dumping *two feet* of rain in one day.

This particular month, September, was the most active period for Atlantic hurricanes. Elena heard about storms everywhere she went.

Four years earlier, the founder of a major Florida corporation bequeathed ACU a sum of fifty million dollars. Since then the university had gone on a building spree. The campus now boasted a new science complex, business school, gym, pool, and dorms. But the president's office remained where it had been, on the ground floor of one of the original structures. The suite of offices was nice enough, though rather faded. Elena decided the place suited the man.

Reed Thompson, president of Atlantic Christian, strode into the room. "Dr. Burroughs! Do we have an appointment?"

"I phoned, your secretary said this was the only chance I'd have to see you today."

"This is excellent. I was hoping to stop by for a chat, but with the trustees meeting next week, I've been running flat out." He accepted the secretary's clutch of messages without breaking stride. "Come on in."

"I can come back later."

"There is no later." He reached the door to his inner office, then asked his secretary, "How much time do I have?"

"Fifteen minutes if you want to arrive five minutes late."

"Make it twenty. Coffee for me. Elena?"

"No thank you."

"Have a seat. Give me two minutes." He hung his jacket on the back of his chair, flipped through the notes, set them by his phone, and seated himself. "How are you settling in?"

"Too early to tell." She found herself slipping into the president's terse mode of speech. "I think okay."

"Any problems?"

"Not with my classes."

"Home working out okay? You're renting, is that right?"

"Bayside Condominiums. Yes, and it's fine. Actually, it's better than that."

"Great." He smiled his thanks as his secretary set down his mug. "You've met Francine?"

"Just now, yes."

His secretary said, "Gary is outside."

"I'll see him in the conference."

"He says there's a problem with the architect's bid."

Reed Thompson sipped from his mug, then said to Elena, "If I take five minutes now, I can give you ten minutes more later. Gary will be able to start the conference without me."

"I feel silly taking your time at all."

"You strike me as someone who does nothing on a whim." He started from the office.

Francine lingered long enough to ask Elena, "Are you sure you won't take anything?"

"A coffee would be great, thank you. Milk, no sugar."

"Just a moment."

Elena looked around the office. She had never had reason to enter the president's office before. Few teachers at a university ever did, with three exceptions: when they were up for a national award, when they were the head of a department undergoing budget battles, and when they were in serious trouble. Elena thanked the secretary for the coffee and wished she had not come. The trouble was, she had nowhere else to turn. She had tried to phone both Lawrence and Antonio, her two friends from the last time events had risen up to strike at her. But both men were unreachable. Ditto for Lawrence's wife. Then the idea had come to her: speak with Reed.

The idea had merit. Reed Thompson had made his name in political economics. Other ACU faculty had told her how Reed had been short-listed for a Nobel Prize. He had served on the Council of Economic Advisers to the first President Bush. Afterward he had turned down several lucrative offers in order to become ACU's president.

The president's office was frigid. She had heard about this, of course. It was a joke among the faculty that anyone visiting the president needed a fur coat. Elena was not surprised. Reed Thompson operated at one speed: full burn. She sipped her coffee and recalled the first time they had met. She had been speaking at Emory University. The event had come at the end of a grueling twelve-week American tour. Elena had arrived drained in body and mind, only to discover that the university had changed the format. Instead of delivering the speech that had become tattooed to her brain, she was to take part in a debate.

Elena wished she could take back that night entirely. She knew now that she should have refused point-blank. But her opponent was Jacob Rawlings, her most ardent critic. The temptation to take him on publicly had been too great.

Jacob Rawlings was extremely handsome and very magnetic. He was every female grad student's dream professor. Which only made it easier to hate him.

Jacob had trained as a behaviorist, which meant he tried to break down the human psyche into rigidly defined components that could be studied and measured and quantified. He loved statistics. He hated what he called the messes of his academic discipline, by which he meant everything that did not fit into a laboratory box. He ridiculed Freud and Jung. Just as, that night, he had mocked Elena.

Jacob had addressed her as *professor*. His tone was polite enough. But his comments had been devastating. He had not merely won the evening's debate; he had obliterated her.

Elena had emerged from the auditorium's stage doors gasping for breath. There she had collided with Reed Thompson, who proceeded to thank her for an astonishing performance.

Elena had been too wounded to give anything other than what was foremost on her mind: "He ate me for lunch."

Reed shrugged easily. "You engaged with him. On his terms. Too many of my colleagues fear the world's ridicule and avoid all such contacts."

"Lucky for them."

"On the contrary. Too often the community of believers engages only with itself, Dr. Burroughs." He offered her a card. "I'm up visiting an old friend who teaches here. He's read your book. I haven't yet, but I will now, I assure you. In the meanwhile, I want you to consider becoming a member of my faculty."

Elena had not been certain she had heard him correctly. "Excuse me?"

"Pray on it. That's all I ask. All anyone can ask." He had offered a brilliant smile, swift as a camera flash. "You would be very good for us, Dr. Burroughs. The question is, would we be good for you?"

"Are you here to tell me you're leaving?"

Elena jerked from her reverie. "What? No. It's nothing like that."

"Because if you are, I won't hold you to your contract." Reed Thompson slipped into the chair. "We were both taking a risk, having you join us. If you don't feel it's working—"

"I'm not here to resign."

He sighed noisily. "Great. Splendid."

She had to smile. "You want me that badly?"

"Well, of course. You think I'd tackle a strange lady in the dead of a Georgia night because I thought she might be interesting?"

"You hardly tackled me."

"In the figurative sense." Reed Thompson was a narrow man in all but his smile and his attitudes. His features were not so much slender as craven, as though he burned through every calorie before it actually hit bottom. "What can I do for you?"

"I need to ask you a question. About economics. It may sound completely silly, but . . ." Elena stopped for a difficult breath. She had it all worked out in her head before she came in, only now the words sounded counterfeit. "Is there a risk of America experiencing a genuine crisis? I'm not talking about another recession. I mean, something truly cataclysmic."

"Absolutely."

The response was so instantaneous, Elena was caught off guard. "Really?"

"The fear of precisely that keeps me up at night."

"Could you explain?"

"May I ask why?"

She had dreaded this question. "I have been approached by a scientist based in Orlando," Elena replied carefully. "She has offered me evidence that has left me extremely disturbed."

"If this evidence has to do with the state of our economy, you have every reason to be disturbed. Terrified, more like. How much do you know about economics?"

"Very little."

"I thought, well, with your previous work with the Oxford council, you would have some training in finance."

She cocked her head. "How did you know about that?"

"I still have my contacts, and I made it my business to learn about your background. Does this have to do with your council work?"

"Not exactly."

"I heard the council had been disbanded."

"It has."

"And that . . . book, the one from your friend."

"*The Book of Dreams.*"

"Is that real?"

"Very much so."

The university president became very still. "Do you have it?"

"When the council disbanded I put it in a safety deposit box. It is still there." She recalled how her friend Miriam had always kept it close at hand, ready to be called upon at any time. Elena had been glad to place it under lock and key. Now, she wondered if she had done the wrong thing.

Elena realized Reed had asked her something, and said, "I'm sorry. I didn't get much sleep. Could you repeat that, please?"

"I said, do you want to tell me the nature of this evidence?"

"Much of it I don't yet understand," Elena said slowly. "But it seemed to suggest a real likelihood of a financial meltdown."

The words catapulted Reed Thompson from his seat. The man's bio said he had been the star of Purdue University's basketball team. He was not tall for a collegiate player, an inch or so over six feet. But his energy was astonishing. "The American economy is always facing risks. There are constant problems. When the housing crisis struck, the people asked, why didn't the government stop this from happening? There are two reasons. First, because the people who were making money from the subprime loan mess were very powerful, and they pressured Washington to look the other way. And second, because the subprime issue was only one of many potential threats to our economy."

Reed began pacing. He moved with catlike grace. His cropped blond hair turned almost transparent as he passed before the window. Elena guessed his age at somewhere around fifty-five. He was handsome in an extremely intense way, but his looks were overshadowed by his energy. He went on, "So in one sense, the situation facing the nation's economy is part of a repetitive pattern. The names have changed, one issue has replaced another. Normally, no one crisis situation is enough to bring down our economy. But today is different."

"We're vulnerable," Elena said.

"Precisely. The nation is barely recovering from the financial debacle brought on us by the subprime crisis. We are in an extremely fragile state. What's more, so are our overseas allies. And together we face a whole string of potentially devastating risks." He stopped and began pointing at items listed on an invisible board. "The European Union is under threat from the economies of Greece, Spain, Ireland, Italy, and Portugal. One or two such problem states they could handle. But if all five default on their loans, the result would be catastrophic for the global economy. And this could well happen. Furthermore, America's housing market is wallowing in unresolved foreclosures. The construction industry has been the driving force of our national growth for decades. It pretty much drew us out of the previous two recessions. Now, builders are hamstrung. Then there is China, which continues to sap our jobs and unbalance our trade revenues by keeping their currency artificially low. And so on. The list of potential dangers, I'm sorry to say, is as long as it has ever been."

Reed dropped his hand to his side, but continued to stare at the invisible board. Finally he turned around and said, "You and your friend have every reason to worry."

"She's not a friend, actually." Elena instantly regretted the comment. It seemed so inane in the face of Reed's seriousness. "I wish I knew what to do."

He walked back behind his desk, but did not resume his seat. "Have you prayed about it?"

"To be honest, my prayer time has seemed pretty hollow recently."

He nodded slowly, as though expecting no other response. "We all go through dry times in our spiritual walk."

His response ignited a gnawing fear in the core of her being. "I'm so worried. Not about the economy. I know that sounds selfish. But it's true. I'm afraid of being dragged back into the public eye."

"Watching you onstage the night we met, I could not recall anyone who looked less pleased to be where she was."

"I positively loathe the spotlight. I always have."

"And yet you entered into a highly public position, one which cost you your job in Oxford as a clinical psychologist. A job which apparently you loved."

"Very much."

"Why did you take on such a task, might I ask?"

She fought against the burning behind her eyes. "Because I felt God was calling me."

He turned toward the window. "While I was in Washington, I joined a prayer group run by Chuck Colson. We met in the White House basement once a week. The group had a transformative effect on my life. When I left public office, I was offered a board position with a Wall Street firm. It would have set me up for life. Instead, I accepted this position. Why? Because God called me to do so." He nodded to the unseen beyond the window. "It has not been easy. And there have certainly been times when the position did not suit me as I might have liked. But in the middle of the night, when I stare at the ceiling and wonder about all the might-have-beens, I know that I did the right thing."

His phone rang. Reed picked it up, said simply, "Coming."

"Thank you for your time." Elena rose from her seat. "I can't tell you how much better I feel than when I arrived."

"In this day and age, Dr. Burroughs, the world would like us to think that people of faith have no place on the global stage. That the time of fervent belief is passed. They would like to relegate us to the dim recesses of half-forgotten myths and superstitions they have outgrown." He showed her a face of stern determination. "That only makes our task more vital."

As Elena left the president's office and crossed the campus to her classroom, she found herself recalling the event that had sealed her first brief meeting with Reed Thompson. Outside the Emory University auditorium, after Reed had asked her to pray about joining the ACU faculty, Elena had been filled with a sensation so strong it had cut through her fatigue and bitter humiliation.

Then, as now, she had known with utter conviction that she could trust this man.

When looking back at the night that followed, it was impossible for Elena to say when the dream started. Her memory of the event was tainted by a sensation that the dream had already existed and was just waiting for the moment when it could pounce. She closed her eyes, and it was there. Crouched in the shadows. She did not even have a chance to fall asleep. It attacked. Immediately.

It started with the faceless man.

In her dream, the doorbell rang. She drifted over and opened the door. The faceless man was there. The messenger in the fine dark suit. He spoke words she did not hear. Instead, she walked back to her bedroom and lay down where she already was. And she dreamed the messenger's tale.

She had been to her Melbourne bank only once before. She had gone there the week of her arrival in Florida to open an account. The bank was far more vivid in her dream than it had been in reality. How crystal clear the image was, how lucid, Elena thought. Everywhere she looked, everything she saw, was etched in almost painful clarity.

A cloying fear entered her dream and mounted with every rising breath, every accelerating heartbeat. She was in a long line waiting before the counter of tellers. Elena turned around. The line where she stood extended out the bank's entrance. She was able to keep her place in line and still see how the line snaked down the street and around the corner and down another block. On and on. Hundreds of people waiting to get inside. Thousands.

Thunder rolled and rumbled, and Elena felt the sound shake her like a leaf. The clouds gathered and the rain fell. None of the people moved. Those who had them simply unfolded umbrellas. All of the umbrellas were black. A crop of dark flowers endured the torrent. Others crouched and shivered. But no one moved. They couldn't. They were as trapped as Elena.

Her attention returned to her place in line as people started moving forward. Her anxiety grew as she approached the counter. She watched the teller deal with the person in front of her. The teller was pleasant enough. Totally detached from the tension and the crowds on the other side of the counter. A man stood behind the line of tellers. He smiled approvingly. As though there was a total disconnect between the bank and the outside world. No storm could touch them. No fear. No panic.

Her turn came. She heard herself say, "I want everything. All my savings. Every cent."

The teller smiled and spoke pleasantly. "Certainly, madame. Here you are."

Elena stared at the pile of shredded bank notes the teller deposited on the counter. "What am I supposed to do with this?"

"Why, whatever you please. It's yours. Take it."

"But it is worthless," Elena heard herself protest.

"Well, you could always use it to start a fire." The teller smiled. "It should burn for quite a while."

4

Elena's hands shook as she poured herself another cup of coffee. The kitchen clock read five past seven. Elena had been up almost two hours.

She picked up the phone and dialed Rachel's cell phone number. The voice mail answered instantly. Elena identified herself and asked Rachel to call her back as soon as possible. She hung up and dialed the number on the back of the card.

The voice that answered did not sound the least bit sleepy. "This is Reggie."

"Elena Burroughs. I'm sorry to call so early."

"Day or night means precisely that, Dr. Burroughs. What can I do for you?"

"I need to speak with Rachel."

"She left for England this morning. She should be landing in . . . six hours and ten minutes. She'll go straight from the airport to a meeting in London. She has a conference call slated for the ride into London. I can ask her to phone you the instant she comes out of the meeting."

"Thank you. Why is she in England?"

"We are planning the global launch of our new drug, Suena-Mind. Rachel is product director." Reginald hesitated, then added, "Quite frankly, Dr. Burroughs, this issue with the dreamer could not have arisen at a worse time."

Elena found a subtle comfort in speaking with Rachel's aide. Though he was worried for different reasons than her own, it was a bond they shared. "What can you tell me about your product?"

"SuenaMind is a totally new treatment for ADHD. Children and adults. The drug is administered as a spray. There are no known side effects."

"None?"

"Not a single adverse reaction has been reported in the three hundred and sixty preliminary trials. Except for the patient with dreams. Which we very much doubt are directly related to our trial. Especially since Rachel's researchers have turned up two others claiming to have precisely the same dreams."

She forced her addled brain to focus. Attention Deficit Hyperactivity Disorder was an enormously hot topic. The majority of medical treatments worked in only a small percentage of patients. And all had potentially grave side effects if taken over a long period. None of the current medications were designed specifically to treat ADHD, primarily because ADHD was the result of several different factors. Some of the causes were biological, others psychological.

"What can you tell me about the other dreamers?"

"We don't know very much yet. Which is why Rachel decided not to include this data in the information she provided you. The morning after she interviewed our test case, that was four days ago, she asked a junior researcher to check and see if anyone else had made such claims. Rachel tells me she actually meant for him to check all the other clinical files. Instead, the researcher did a global Internet search and turned up two others making what appear to be identical claims. One lives in Ottawa, the other in Washington. Neither has ever had any connection to our company."

Elena struggled to make sense of the information. "What is your drug's success rate?"

"Close to a hundred percent."

"Is it a cure?"

"We've been specifically ordered to avoid using this word in association with our product, Dr. Burroughs."

"Of course. I understand."

"What we can say is, SuenaMind is groundbreaking in every sense of the word. This time next year, Rachel Lamprey could be both famous and rich."

"What about you?"

If Reginald Pierce felt any discomfort over her question, he did not show it. "You're asking why I would serve as Rachel's PA?"

The man was as observant as he was handsome. "You do seem overqualified."

"I'm the second person to hold this position. My predecessor went on to become a vice president of SuenaMed. Rachel has asked me to stay for two years. Night and day. Your basic corporate servitude. When it's over, the sky is the limit. Rachel delivers."

"How long have you been with her?"

"Ten months. To tell the truth, I'll be sorry when my time is up. She is an amazing lady."

Elena heard the unspoken. "Rachel's interest in dreams does not fit her profile."

"Rachel lives for her work. She is as driven as anyone I have ever met." Reginald Pierce hesitated a long moment, then added, "We're approaching critical mass here. The marketing and publicity departments are gearing up for a global release. Our first-year sales of this product are expected to be over three billion dollars. Now, she's been blindsided by this. When every second counts. The future of our company is riding on this product and its launch." A hint of Elena's own panic entered the young man's voice. "Can you help her?"

Elena shook her head in denial to the man she could not see. "I was actually calling to ask the same question."

His tone instantly became guarded. "What's the matter?"

"I've had the dream."

"What, the same one that our clinical patient reported?"

"Exactly the same."

The kitchen clock ticked softly through the silence. Elena's brain flashed through dream images, and she felt her heart race the seconds.

Reginald asked, "Could this be the result of the power of suggestion?"

"I've been asking myself the same thing. It is certainly possible. But the force of this experience . . ."

"It was as intense as what the man described?"

"I felt as though I had entered a second reality." She swallowed against the gnawing terror. And something more. "Ever since I woke up, I have felt a burning need to tell people."

"Just like the patient reported." Reginald Pierce almost groaned the words.

Elena used the sleeve of her robe to wipe the perspiration from her forehead. "I've never known such intensity. I'm a trained professional. I cannot fathom how this sense of urgency could be derived from observing a patient describe his symptoms. I have treated patients for years without ever having such a reaction."

"This is so totally not good." Reginald's sigh rattled the phone. "I will have Rachel call you the instant she lands."

The phone rang so swiftly after she hung up, Elena assumed it was Reginald again. She answered with a simple "Yes?"

"Tell me I haven't woken you up."

"Vicki?"

"I knew I should have waited. But believe me, hon, this was too good to keep."

Vicki Ferrell was her New York editor, a woman who sheathed her razor edges in Gucci and Ferragamo. She was a Valkyrian queen of fire and ice. Her voice carried a natural force that could launch or destroy careers from half a world away. She was a passionate follower of opera and French cuisine. Above all, however, she was constantly in pursuit of the next global bestseller. Her stable of authors was legendary. Elena knew full well what would happen the instant her book faded. Unless she produced another hit, she would be erased without a backward glance. New York publishing had no time for has-beens. Concern over yesterday's friendships was left on the Jersey shore. Even so, Elena found Vicki both charming and irresistible. It was also nearly impossible to tell the woman no.

Elena declared, "I'm not doing any more public appearances."

"Do you hear me asking? No, you do not. Can't a girl just get in touch, see how my favorite author is surviving in the Florida swamps and gators?"

Elena felt the bundle of tension that had gnawed at her begin to ease. Vicki had the power to cut through anything else the day might hold. "I haven't seen any of either."

"What about mosquitoes? I hear they're big enough to carry off mobile homes."

"You don't call unless you want something. What is it this time?"

"Hon, I want to make your day."

Elena decided it had to be a sweetened offer for a new book. Elena wanted to turn Vicki down before the woman started her pitch. But one glance around the rented condo's tawdry kitchen forced her to say, "I'm listening."

"I got an e-mail this morning from your nemesis. None other than Professor Jacob Rawlings."

"What?"

"I know. Talk about your basic bombshell. He also phoned my cell. Eight times. When we spoke, he claims he got my number from the Emory president. Another name to add to my scalp list."

"Jacob Rawlings called and e-mailed you. About me."

"Right. To say he's sorry for how he treated you during the debate, and how they managed to blindside you by his appearance. He apologized and he apologized. It was almost an aria." The words carried barely suppressed laughter. "We pause while the world famous author picks herself up off the floor."

Elena had the feeling that she was running after the conversation, unable to catch up. "Is this some kind of joke?"

"You betcha. The best kind. One that's true. Hon, I'm telling you, the man was on his knees. It was delicious. Desperation dripped from his every word. The man actually begged. He needs you to check out something on the Internet. Got a pen?"

And Elena thought the day could not hold any more surprises. "Hold on. Okay."

"He asks you to check out a secure website." Vicki read out an Internet address, then, "Password is 'urgent hyphen urgent,' no spaces. He's ready to crawl over a bed of hot coals if you'll spare him five minutes. He left a number."

"Jacob Rawlings expects me to call him."

"I know. The nerve." The suppressed laughter almost broke through. "The only thing that would have shocked me more would be hearing you've started work on your new book."

"I'm hanging up now."

"Girl, you have *got* to call me back the instant you're done roasting the man."

Elena had a sudden urge to tell Vicki about the dream and the warning. The aching need penetrated so fiercely she had to fight to hang up the phone.

Jacob Rawlings's encrypted website was actually a hidden component of the best-known forum used by clinical psychologists. Elena had attended numerous web conferences here. She had posted her own lectures and articles. But she had not known such a confidential side-area even existed. She typed the location into the empty search box in the site's top right corner. Beneath it appeared a second box, requesting a password. She hesitated a long moment, fearing this invasion of her professional world by a man she loathed. Elena sighed, defeated by morbid curiosity, and entered the password, "urgent-urgent."

Before her appeared a blank white screen showing a series of five electronic files. Each file was labeled simply, "Clinical Study," and numbered. Below each was a date, time, and location. All of the dates were from the previous seventy-two hours. The locations gave her pause. The first file was from Atlanta. The second, New York City. The third, Montreal. Then Tokyo. And Christchurch, New Zealand.

She clicked on the first file and found herself staring at Jacob Rawlings. His face filled the screen as he adjusted the camera's position. Even distorted by his proximity to the lens, the man remained both magnetic and extremely handsome. His hair was a coppery blend of red and blond. His features were even, his gaze penetrating. Even his frown was attractive.

An unseen woman said nervously, "I don't see what possible good this can do."

Elena felt a macabre fascination in observing Jacob Rawlings in his office. It was like tracking the beast to its lair. She watched him walk in front of the camera and settle behind his desk. "I would like to share your experience with a trusted colleague."

Elena backed away from her computer screen. The man could not possibly have been referring to her.

The woman asked, "Who is this person?"

"Dr. Elena Burroughs was formerly at Oxford. Now she's in Florida. She's a recognized authority on dream states. Perhaps you read her bestseller, *The Book of Dreams*."

"No." The woman was square and heavy in a manner that defied her elegant dress and makeup. "I can't possibly have strangers discussing my personal affairs."

"Dr. Burroughs is a highly trained clinician with a great deal more familiarity with dreams than myself. She is utterly trustworthy. I can assure you, this will go no further." When the patient remained silent, crouched in the chair on the desk's opposite side, Jacob went on, "You wanted to share this experience with the world, isn't that what you told me?"

"I don't *want* to. I *must*. I am *compelled*."

"Think of this as a way to satisfy your urges, while retaining a very real confidentiality."

"I suppose . . ."

"Let's start with a few personal details. Your age?"

"Fifty-seven."

"Your current professional status?"

"I hold the Lloyd Chair of Finance at Emory. I am also a member of the Federal Reserve Bank of Atlanta."

"Your marital status?"

"I am married to my husband of thirty-six years. Four children and two grandchildren."

"Have you ever before sought professional help or counseling for any psychiatric issue?"

"No. Never."

His chair creaked as he leaned forward. "Would you please repeat what you have related to me about your dreams."

"First of all, I didn't have dreams. There has been just one. But repeated every night. And second, I'm not sure it was a dream at all."

"How would you describe the experience, then?"

She was silent for a very long time, then, "I have no idea."

5

Elena taught the day's three classes in a haze. Images from the previous night came and went in emotional waves. Twice she was almost overwhelmed by the urge to shriek her warning to the students. She maintained a grip only by turning to the board and clamping down, just clenching up from her toes to her creased forehead. She recalled how her addicted patients described the sudden lurching need to inject or ingest or sniff their drug of choice. The struggle to resist. How they had to hold tight and ride it out. Elena had never truly understood what they meant until now.

Between classes was no better. She reviewed the five electronic files again. The people were quite different, but their patterns were astonishingly similar. The term was *clinically parallel*. This signified case histories in which, when individual traits were removed, the underlying symptoms were identical. Elena was not concerned when the Montreal patient spoke French and the elderly Tokyo man spoke Japanese. She scanned the attached written translations for deviations, and found none.

Elena's phone rang five minutes before the end of her final class. She had left it open on her desk, in case Rachel called. The phone's readout said "International." Elena released her students and answered.

Rachel's first words were, "Did you review the material?"

"Yes. Can you talk?"

"I'm in the back of a Rolls limo. The only problem with a Rolls is, they're too comfortable. I want to sleep. But I can't. Reginald says he explained what we're up against with the global release of SuenaMind."

"He did, yes."

"This is the make-or-break moment for us. Today we're doing the final run-through for simultaneous launches in all of Western Europe."

"Perhaps we should leave this for another time."

"If you have studied the material, you know that is not an option." Rachel hesitated, then said, "Reginald tells me you had the dream."

"Last night."

"Was this . . . I'm sorry, I don't know—"

"Psychosomatic stress disorder. Most definitely not."

"How can you be so sure?"

"I have been a practicing clinician for eight years. In that time, I've never experienced an empathetic reaction to a patient's description of their symptoms."

"There is always a first time."

"Not like this." Elena felt the gnawing ache grip her middle. "The dream was exactly as your patient described. Too vivid to be called a dream at all. And afterward . . ."

"Yes?"

"I have had to fight down a desperate need to tell the world."

The silence crackled with distance and a frisson of tension. Finally Rachel said, "I'm speechless."

"I somehow find that comforting."

"Very few things surprise me."

"Here's another. This morning I received a message from an arch skeptic of dream analysis, a man I personally loathe. Dr. Jacob Rawlings is a clinician and professor at Emory. He has reported another five cases. All have taken place in the past few days. They are spread all over the globe. Tokyo, New Zealand, Montreal. Three are senior corporate officials. One is a leading politician. Another is a politician's wife. Their dream patterns are remarkably similar. All within the range of what you would classify as standard deviations. The bank, the line, the shredded currency, the need to share this with others. All there."

Rachel's voice had dropped a full octave when she responded. "Can you forward me the files?"

"I'll have to ask Jacob's permission. Knowing the man, I doubt he will agree."

"He has to."

"He will want some kind of official assurance the information goes no further. We may have to wait until waivers are signed. There are legal issues and different national—"

"Please stress to him the urgency."

"You may have to settle for written transcripts."

"Only if absolutely necessary. Tell him our legal team is at his disposal." Rachel accepted this with bad grace. "The car is pulling up to my next appointment. I have to go, Elena. One more thing. Reginald has just reported rumors of a bank crisis. I've told him to contact you with any details. I'm flying back immediately after this conference, so let's talk tomorrow, yes? And try and convince your colleague that we need access to those testimonials."

"There's one thing more," Elena said.

Rachel's voice grew quite weak. "More?"

"I need you to contact your patient. Ask him how his dream

began." Elena ran through a brief description of the faceless messenger in her own dream.

"Just a moment."

Elena heard Rachel's muffled voice telling the driver to circle the block. Then, "The man from our trial has disappeared."

"When?"

"We're not . . . His wife reports he never returned from the taping session in my office."

"That was days ago."

"Four. No, sorry, it's five now. Transatlantic travel and time change. Forgive me. We only just learned this morning."

"How is that possible?"

"Our clinical trials are in their third phase. Do you understand what this means? The patients are released. They interact with their natural environments. They return once a week for monitoring. Every two weeks they receive their next dose and are retested. Up to this case, there have been *no* adverse reactions."

"What do you know about him?"

"Almost nothing. He is a plumber, he runs his own small business based in Ocala. His wife reported him missing the next day. Generally the police give adults at least seventy-two hours before listing them as official missing persons. The wife apparently contacted our office as soon as she heard this. But the buffoons running our corporate security did not think to pass it on until this morning. I would be taking heads if I was not so overwhelmed by everything."

"The police have no leads?"

"They have felt no urgency. That is about to change, I assure you." Rachel sighed. "I've been so desperately worried. I can't tell you how relieved I am to learn you have experienced this dream."

Elena's shudder creased her reply: "I'm not."

.   .   .

As soon as she cut the connection with Rachel, Elena dialed Jacob Rawlings's office. She did not want to wait. Her resolve might weaken, and this call had to happen. But when the faculty secretary said he was traveling and would not return for three days, Elena heaved a great sigh of relief.

The secretary asked, "Who is calling, please?"

"My name is Elena Burroughs, and—"

"Oh, Dr. Burroughs, thank goodness. Dr. Rawlings waited here until the very last moment, it's a wonder he caught his plane." The secretary had a honeyed Georgia voice, one that would have been quite pleasant except for the person they discussed. "He is scheduled to deliver a talk tonight. At a meeting of behaviorists at the Peabody Orlando."

"Dr. Rawlings is in Orlando?"

"For tonight and all day tomorrow. He is then flying to Washington. He is so eager to speak with you. I can't tell you how important it is. I'm sorry, but he didn't say precisely what it was about."

"I was sent some files to review."

"They must be important. Why, the man wore a hole in my carpet, pacing around my desk. As if hovering and giving us all a case of the nerves would make you call him any faster."

"Do you have a number where I can reach him?"

"Oh my, yes. For his cell phone and his hotel both." She read off the numbers. "Wait, let me pull up his schedule. The opening event started half an hour ago. I'm sorry, he'll be seated on the podium. Which means his phone will be shut off."

"When will the convocation end tonight?"

"They break for dinner at seven thirty. If they're on time. Which they never are. I'm sure if you were to call him in a couple of hours he could slip away. He was so concerned, Dr. Burroughs. I really do think it would be best not to wait an instant longer."

•　　•　　•

Elena prepared and ate a solitary evening meal. She was seated on the stool pulled up to the kitchen counter. The dining room table had not been used once since she moved in. A small flat-screen television stood in the corner where the counter met the wall. The evening news kept her company. The newscaster described rumors of a London bank failure.

Elena reached for the remote and turned up the volume. The business correspondent was reporting live across the street from a bank: "The problem with such rumors is being played out before our very eyes. A bank that was apparently healthy as of yesterday is now threatened with ruin. The bank run you see behind me threatens to become a self-fulfilling panic."

Behind the newscaster stood a line of customers that stretched from the bank entrance down the length of the sidewalk, before disappearing around the corner.

"The fact that all deposits have been guaranteed by the Bank of England has not stopped these depositors from desperately seeking to withdraw their funds. One unnamed source claims the bank has seen a net extraction of eighty-nine million pounds in the last four hours of business. If this continues, the bank will be stripped bare of assets by the end of this week."

As Elena watched, it began to rain at the scene. Those who had come prepared opened umbrellas. The others cowered and shivered in the downpour. The business correspondent went on: "Given the British economy's current fragile state, this run on the bank represents far more than the uncertainty felt by the general public. Such events could well threaten the nation's economic health, and destabilize its recovery."

When the station broke for commercial, Elena turned off the television. She entered the kitchen and scraped the remainder of her half-finished meal into the garbage. What she had eaten sat in her stomach like lead.

She took her phone out on the balcony. The sky was split by a pair of storms. Dark walls obliterated her view of the water both to the north and south. Directly ahead was a pyrotechnical sunset display. The rumbles of thunder formed a bass resonance as she dialed the number.

He answered before the first ring was finished: "Rawlings."

"It's Elena Burroughs."

"Oh, thank goodness. Wait a moment. I have to leave the stage."

Of all the things she might have expected to hear from Jacob, heartfelt gratitude did not make the list. She turned on the fan, and felt the air push at the cloying heat.

Jacob Rawlings came back on. "Did you review the files?"

"I did, yes. But there's more." She swiftly related Rachel Lamprey's documented patient.

Jacob responded with a silence so intense she could almost feel the man's concentration. "Can you come to Orlando?"

"I have a ten o'clock class, and another at noon, then my day is free. The trip shouldn't take more than an hour and a half."

"I'm due to speak again at two. I can't get out of it. I should be done by three thirty. Do you know the convention center?"

"I'm sure I can find it."

"The Peabody is directly across the street from the main hall." He hesitated, then said, "Dr. Burroughs, if you will permit, I will wait and apologize to you in person."

"All right." She tasted the lingering flavor of words not yet spoken. "Are you in contact with the other clinicians?"

"I certainly can be. Why?"

"I need you to ask if any of the patients experienced a faceless messenger at the beginning of their dream."

"I can tell you my own patient reported nothing of the sort."

"Their recollection might be vague. Perhaps because of this they assume it was part of an earlier dream." Elena felt a sudden pressing need to share this image with someone else, even a stranger on the other side of the world. "A stranger in a dark suit who has no face, and whose words can't be heard."

"Why are you asking me to do this, Dr. Burroughs?"

"Because my own started that way."

"Sorry, you're telling me you've found a patient of your own?"

"No." She stopped, held by a sudden fear that his ridicule might return, and be stronger still. But she had no choice. "I have had the same dream."

There was a sharp intake of breath. "I *knew* it was right to contact you about this. I *knew* it." Then, "Have you seen the news about the London bank?"

"I was just watching it." She decided there was no reason not to add, "It was raining in my dream."

He huffed a single breath. "I will be waiting for you in the lobby."

Elena cut off the kitchen lights and retreated to her bedroom. She had positioned a secondhand desk by the window, facing out over the water. She opened her laptop and drew up the picture of a page from *The Book of Dreams*. The images came from a book given to her by Miriam, the friend who had died the previous summer. Miriam had received the original book and five ancient copies from her own great-grandmother. The line of possession stretched back through time to the realm of myth and impossible age. The copies and the original all contained images drawn in Aramaic cuneiform. Each image was formed from a line of the Lord's Prayer.

Before Elena had left on her book tour, she had returned all of the books to her safety deposit box. Before then, however, she had photographed the pages so they could travel with her. Several times over the long summer she had raised the images and tried to enter into what the early church leaders once called a contemplative state. The images had previously helped intensify her prayer life. But all through that weary summer, Elena had felt nothing. Just like now. The only thing that came to her through the picture was a stronger sense of the storm gathering beyond her apartment.

Elena cut off the computer and opened the drawer by her bed. Despite the trauma she had endured around the time of the book's arrival, she had gained a number of vital insights. And one of them was that the book itself was nothing. The only purpose the book held, the only value, was in drawing the viewer closer to God. And she did not need the book to do that. She never had.

Elena had felt that the time for the book's practical application had ended; that moment and that particular purpose lay in the past. Now, as Elena examined the image, she wondered if its time had come again.

Elena opened her Bible to the book of Daniel. Her fingers found the place before she consciously knew what she sought. But there it was before her eyes, a vivid reminder of another man given the unwanted responsibility. Elena read the opening passage and felt an easing away of her stress and her worry. No matter what else, she was not alone. She never had been. Not for an instant.

When the phone rang, she was tempted not to answer. But then she saw the readout and knew she had to take the call. She pressed the button and said, "Vicki, I'm so sorry."

"I've been wondering if maybe I did something worse than usual, to have you not call me back."

"No, no, it's just this day became a little overwhelming."

"Did you talk to the man?"

"An hour ago."

"And?"

"I'm driving to Orlando after class tomorrow to meet him."

"Do you need my gun?"

"No, thank you. You own a gun?"

"Hey. I'm a single lady, and this is Manhattan." Vicki's voice took on a delicious edge. "Did you two kiss and make up?"

"I'm hanging up now."

"Not before you promise me a book from all this mess."

"Mess is right," Elena replied.

It seemed as though she had only just turned out her light when the next dream began.

The faceless messenger rang her doorbell. Elena did not want to open the door. She fought against moving forward, as strongly as she had struggled against anything in her whole life. For whatever the dream might reveal, however vital the images might prove, she did not want them. She did not want to be filled anew with dread. She did not want her life to slip even further from her control.

But she answered the door anyway. She had no choice. It was, after all, a dream.

The faceless messenger was as well dressed as before. She could clearly see the fine cut to his suit, the polish to his shoes. Even the lovely design in his knitted silk tie. His cuff links flashed as he lifted a hand toward her. Offering something she did not want. He spoke, and she recognized his voice from the previous time. But his words were just as unclear as before. Even so, they rocked her. She saw nothing of his face. There was a round gray cloud where his features should have been. The voice emerged from this vague cloud, and pummeled her. She shut the door, and instantly the next phase of the dream attacked. Her whole being was assaulted by its force.

Only it was not the same dream as before.

It was something else entirely.

And it was far, far worse.

6

The Peabody Hotel in Orlando was surrounded on three sides by one of the nation's largest convention centers. Elena left her car with the parking attendant and entered a vast lobby of granite and bronze sculptures. As she passed the concierge desk, she noticed how most of the people crowding the lobby were watching a television suspended from the rear wall. Elena drew in close enough to hear the newscaster describe how the previous day's London bank run had continued to develop overnight, impacting shares of every bank listed on the British exchanges. They replayed images from the Lehman Brothers' collapse several years earlier: the thousands of bank employees leaving the crippled establishment with their professional lives in cardboard boxes, and the pandemonium that had struck the international markets. As she turned away, Elena saw the tense and worried faces, and felt the dreams assault her once more.

Jacob Rawlings was moving toward her as she emerged from the crowd. "Dr. Burroughs, you came."

"I said I would."

"Well, yes. But I couldn't help but have my doubts."

The tension trailed along with her as they left the lobby and entered a grand central chamber. "I didn't want to come," she confessed. "I had no choice in the matter."

"Honesty. Excellent. I agree that we should do our best to move on." He gestured to a pair of cane chairs by a glass table. "Would this do? Or, if you prefer, I could try and arrange a private meeting room."

"This is fine." She could not tell if her own apprehension resulted from the television images or the proximity of her former nemesis. All Elena knew was, she wasn't about to be alone with this man.

Jacob Rawlings was far more handsome than she recalled. Which was hardly a surprise, since they had spent most of their one highly public encounter shouting at each other. He was also very courtly. He held her chair, then hovered by her side as he asked, "Would you care to freshen up?"

"No, thank you. Let's get started."

"What about a coffee? Or tea, perhaps. I could arrange sandwiches, a light lunch?"

"Later, perhaps." She pointed at the chair beside her. "Sit. Please."

He launched into his apology before planting himself in the seat. "I can't tell you how sorry I am for what I said at our debate. In light of present events, I feel like such a total fool."

"I appreciate your comments, Dr. Rawlings—"

"Please, call me Jacob."

"But words are cheap." Elena had spent the entire journey up deciding upon what she was about to say. "I was publicly flayed by your hand. Your scorn still burns."

Their antagonism had not started with the unexpected debate. Jacob Rawlings had been one of her book's most vociferous critics. He had written a scathing review carried by two key journals, one in the US and the other in England. He had then publicly lambasted her at a professional conference, one that she thankfully had not attended. She only learned about it following the Emory debate. She had made a point of not paying attention to such things, especially since Vicki had sheltered her from most negative publicity. Then had come the Emory debacle. Elena considered it her own fault for not having been better prepared, as Jacob certainly had been. Even so, the memories still burned.

Elena went on, "I want three things. First, you will write a letter to be published in the next issue of *Psychology Today*, expressing your deep regret for your previous stand. And that in light of new evidence, you have decided to retract your statements and come fully around to my perspective on dream analysis."

Jacob Rawlings took this in. The retraction would be a major event among her professional colleagues. That spring he had been appointed to the journal's editorial board. Even so, he slowly nodded. "Agreed."

"Second, you will arrange a public forum, preferably at Emory but another major assembly will do. You will renounce your former position. You will apologize to me publicly. And then we will engage not in a debate but in a dialogue. On where dream analysis should go next, and how it can be fit into the mainstream of psychological study."

She saw the subtle shudder, saw him repress it. And found herself reluctantly admiring the inner resolve this represented. Jacob nodded again. "And third?"

"You will come up with something on your own. A gesture of your own making."

She almost regretted this third idea. It sounded almost petty as she spoke the words. She was about to tell him to forget it, when he said thoughtfully, "I was invited to speak at the national convocation of behaviorists. I had decided to turn it down. I will accept, and I will use the platform to discuss your concepts in a positive light."

It was Elena's turn to feel pushed back into her chair. Behaviorists were the most rigid of all psychologists. Jacob had started his career, done his initial studies, at a university dedicated to behaviorism and the determination to make psychology a science. Which meant stripping down everything about the mental process into tightly measurable phenomena. There were a multitude of problems with this. Behaviorists shunned anything to do with emotions. One of their principal tenets held that virtually all human behavior was based upon genetic makeup and measurable physical and environmental factors. Past traumatic experiences or emotional states were considered both superficial and subject to change, and so should be discounted. Dreams were an anathema to behaviorists. For one of their own, risen to the ranks of national stardom, to discuss dream analysis at their national gathering would have the impact of a hydrogen bomb.

Elena said softly, "Thank you, Jacob."

His smile carried genuine relief. "Does this mean we can now move on?"

"Yes." She wished she had the ability just then to return his smile. Perhaps another time. One when she was not required to say, "I've had another dream."

Jacob Rawlings paced the foyer on the other side of the fountain. As he talked into his cell phone, a growing number of very young children gathered near him with their mothers. Many of the women gave Jacob lingering glances. Elena could well understand why.

Three years earlier, Jacob had been tapped to host a three-part series on childhood development for the Discovery Channel. There had been a good many chuckles over the news when it first broke, as Jacob had never married. But the program had been a surprise hit, drawing the highest numbers of any cable-network fact-based program for the entire year. Elena had watched an episode once, and despite her resentment over his scathing review of her book, she had been forced to admit the man had a magnetic quality.

A recent analysis of successful movie stars had resulted in a remarkable discovery. The study had concluded that an actor's talent and general attractiveness were only part of the equation. Of great importance was what the scientists termed as *physical equilibrium*. By this they meant the actor possessed almost ideal proportions. They had compared a number of stars to a computer image of perfect form—stance, balance, shape of head and shoulders, and so forth. Both the male and female viewers tended to be drawn toward the person who represented the ideal physical form, rating them higher than those typically considered more attractive.

As Elena watched him pace the foyer's inlaid marble floor, she decided that Jacob Rawlings possessed both looks and balance. Not to mention intelligence. She found herself enjoying the sight. He was, she decided, almost too good a package. She had recently seen his photograph somewhere, a lovely blond model with a vacant gaze on his arm. The model had been signed as the new face for Lancôme cosmetics. Elena had decided the two probably deserved each other.

Jacob paced and continued a conversation so grimly intense he remained blind to the attention being cast his way. Elena leaned back in her seat, wearied by the day and the night before. Against her will, she found herself being drawn back into the dream's vivid images.

The dream had carried with it a sense of jarring disconnect. As though reality was undergoing a seismic shift, one only she could see. The world tilted on its axis, and only she had a compass and could detect the coming tumult.

The feelings of anxiety and pending disaster had been far stronger than the images themselves. If anything, the view had been almost benign, especially compared to the bank's interior. Elena had left an office where she had formerly held a job. She joined a line, which quickly grew along the street. They did not march in step. They shuffled.

As the dream continued, the line of people became a flood. They filled the street from one side to the other. They grew increasingly packed together. And still more came, piling in from all the doorways and offices and side streets.

The crowd became so dense she could not draw a decent breath. She struggled, yet at the same time remained vaguely docile. She knew it was vital that she not lose her place in line. If she made a scene, she would be sent to the back. And that would be terrible. Why, she wasn't sure. But she knew she had to behave if she wanted to remain where she was.

With each step the crowd's forward progress moved more slowly. The people turned a final corner. Elena felt a growing sense of desperation, as though she caught the smell of something on the unseen wind, and knew she was nearly there. Finally she was able to see what awaited her down that street.

Ahead of her was a single narrow door. Everyone wanted to enter. Everyone tried desperately to hide their frantic impatience. They shuffled forward, and the closer they came the greater her anxiety grew. Just as her tension rose to a fever pitch, she noticed a woman standing beside the door. The woman's voice was eerily calm. She spoke in a soft cadence, totally disconnected from what surrounded her.

"Keep your place in line," the woman chanted. "One person at a time through the door. Take your time. There is soup enough for everyone."

Two stone buildings formed the cavern that trapped her. Both walls held billboards covered with the same newspaper headline. The boards read GLOBAL STOCK MARKETS NOSEDIVE.

The closer Elena came to that awful door, the more certain she became. The woman's words were a lie. There wasn't enough. There never would be again.

Jacob ended the call just as four liveried attendants placed a set of miniature stairs by the fountain's edge and unfurled a narrow red carpet. He watched askance as the ducks waddled down the stairs and paraded across the carpet. Mothers and daughters cooed as the ducks entered the elevator. A sign was placed by the fountain, saying that the ducks had gone in for their afternoon naps.

Jacob returned to their table and said, "Did that just happen?"

"Every day, apparently."

He swept a copper-blond strand from his forehead. "This meeting certainly holds a surreal edge."

"Who was that on the phone?"

As soon as she had finished relating her dream, Jacob had leapt to his feet, excused himself, taken his phone from his pocket, and started pacing. Jacob replied, "My patient."

"The Federal Reserve bank board member?"

"The same." He swept his forehead again, only this time there was no hair out of place. He did not notice. "Her name is Agatha Hune. She was referred to me three years ago with a stress-related disorder. She attended counseling sessions for six months. I consider her a friend. The woman is extremely intelligent, well balanced, with an honest perspective on life and her issues. As you can imagine, this whole situation has been extremely distressing."

Something in the way he spoke led Elena to surmise, "She has had the same dream, hasn't she? The second one."

Jacob's response was halted by the ringing of his phone. He glanced at the readout and said, "I need to take this."

"Go ahead."

He took one step away and turned his back to her, but only for a moment. When he turned back around, his gaze held the same frantic edge Elena had seen in the mirror that morning.

Jacob shut the phone and said, "That was my closest friend from university. Bob Meadows is a clinical psychologist in Miami."

The tense way he spoke those words told her all she needed to know. "There's been another dreamer, hasn't there."

Jacob nodded. "For the first time in my professional career, I have no idea what to do next."

7

Rachel Lamprey's call came while they waited for Elena's car to be brought around. Rain fell in silver sheets from the hotel's overhang. There was no wind, not a breath. Though the day was still warm, the mist gave off a chilling taste. From somewhere beyond the liquid curtain, lightning flashed and thunder rolled.

Rachel had to shout to be heard. "Where are you?"

"Orlando. But we're—"

"Excellent! I've just landed in New York. I have a meeting here in the first-class lounge, then I'm due back into Orlando around nine tonight. Can we meet?"

"I'm headed to Miami."

"What on earth for?"

The woman's sharp tone surprised Elena. It shouldn't have; Elena had noted the bossy edge lurking beneath Rachel's polished surface. But she had assumed she was protected from Rachel's wrath. Elena replied, "Jacob's site has received a new hit. A psychiatrist in Miami has a new patient who has experienced both dreams." Elena realized she had not mentioned the latest experience, and added, "Last night I had another dream. It has struck all the others as well. Jacob was confirming this—"

"I know all about the second dream," Rachel said impatiently. "Why is Jacob involved?"

The attendant pulled through the rain and halted beside Elena. She tipped him and nodded her thanks as he held her door. "Jacob Rawlings is . . . a professional associate."

Jacob heard her hesitation, and offered her a rueful smile as he climbed in and shut his door.

"Whatever or whoever is waiting in Miami is *certainly* not as important as our meeting tonight!"

"With respect, Rachel, I don't agree. We have not been told this new patient's name. Jacob is friends with the psychologist involved. They have spoken. We've been assured the patient holds enormous—"

"Do you have any idea how far out on a limb I have gone to include you?" Rachel's heat was so blistering, the phone felt hot to the touch. "We have got to speak *tonight.*"

Behind her, a horn beeped politely. Elena put the car in gear and pulled forward. Rain drummed on the roof. "We are talking now, Rachel."

"What is that *noise*?"

"Another thunderstorm. Tell me what is the matter."

"Can you *possibly* be asking me that question? You, of all people? This is not the time for *clinical analysis.* This is time for *action.* Have you even *seen* the reports of the London bank run?"

"Yes, I have." Elena retreated from the rage as she had a thousand times before, stepping back from a patient's distress and emotional tirade. Refusing to be drawn in. Allowing her the distance required for her to hear beneath the surface. The woman's anger became just another drumming cadence upon her professional shell, not touching her any more than the rain. "But that is not the issue, is it?"

"What?"

"There is something else at work. Another problem that has wreaked havoc in your day." Elena paused, then asked, "Do you want to tell me about it?"

"In person," Rachel snapped.

"Then it will need to wait until tomorrow."

"It can't."

"Do you want to tell me why?"

Rachel was silent for a long moment, then cut the connection.

The rain ended with startling suddenness. The turnpike swiftly dried. The heat shimmered above open fields and wild palms and broad ponds and tall emerald grass. Jacob had not spoken since they left the hotel. Abruptly he said, "I have a patient who lost his father three months ago. They were extremely close. Since then he has become obsessed with the Weather Channel. He starts every session by updating me on the hurricane season."

"He should move to Melbourne," Elena said. "The local channel updates the weather every ten minutes around the clock. With the hurricane's approach, the weather reports have grown so long they merge into one another."

"People feel a desperate need to find some mythical control over their own destinies," Jacob mused. "In earlier times, it was superstition and charms. Now it's information. They subconsciously believe this will allow them to influence the outcome. If only they know enough, and far enough in advance."

Elena glanced over. "You're not religious, are you?"

"My father was a Presbyterian minister. We relocated eleven times before I left for university. I attended six different high schools. I hated it. At some visceral level, I still resent what my father's faith put us through."

"Is that your answer?"

"It is very hard for me to separate my past from any discussion of God." He drummed his fingernails on the side window. "That was one of the things that most rankled me about your book. How you repeatedly hinted at a connection between dreams and the divine."

"You have still not answered my question."

He sighed. "When I was young, I believed because it was expected of me. When I went to university, I left it all behind."

"I think it is precisely because of the divine connection within some dreams that we will never understand their full scope until this relationship is acknowledged."

"I have not seen any indication that the recipients of these dreams are religious."

Elena repeated the word: "Recipient."

"What else would you call them? Tell me, please. I'm desperate to find another word to describe them."

"Why, Jacob, because it hints at a connection beyond the measurable? Because it suggests a greater force is at work?" When he did not reply, Elena went on: "There are a number of places in the Bible where dreams come to people who do not believe in God. That is not the critical issue. What is vital is that the *interpreter* be a person of faith. God grants to some a special gift. They hold the power to explain his message. This is why I feel faith has a vital role to play. Not just in dreams. But in the individual's overall health and in the treatment of any number of disorders. So long as psychologists avoid the issue of faith, they cut themselves off from an entire portion of the human psyche."

"My father would certainly agree with you," Jacob said. His tone was flat, his expression fixed.

"So how would you suggest we proceed?"

He pondered this through several miles. Finally he replied, "I feel we should focus on the one central point that we can now prove. A collection of individuals who have never met, who are separated by vast distances, are all being affected by the same dream."

"'Affected' is too weak to describe the experience. The dreamer is *assaulted*," Elena replied. Jacob's unwillingness to include faith was not so much a vacuum as a path not taken. But arguing over this would get them nowhere. There was nothing, however, keeping her from having a running discourse with herself. Which she did. For the remainder of their three-hour journey, she talked with Jacob on one level, and prayerfully dialogued on another.

The traffic around Miami was awful. Jacob had been there often enough, for reasons he saw no need to explain. Which Elena took to signify that a woman was involved. Without his guidance she doubted they would ever have arrived at their destination. He directed her down small palm-lined roads, through a subdivision of one-story concrete bungalows, until they turned onto the main shopping street of Coral Gables. They halted in front of the Ritz-Carlton, an upscale hotel of brick and glass that was built to resemble an Aztec pyramid, right down to the hanging vines that tumbled down the stepping-stone structure.

They followed the instructions passed on by Jacob's colleague, and took the elevator to the top floor. A portly young man was seated where the elevators opened into the main hallway, talking softly into his phone and making rapid notes. He held up one finger, signaling for them to wait. The young man did not appear to have a single sharp edge to his body. Even his voice was soft, a melodious tone that lingered on each word. Elena decided his patients probably all loved him for his voice. Every word seemed to carry the promise of comfort.

He shut the phone and stood. "Forgive me. That was a patient I had to cancel because of the issue bringing us together. Dr. Burroughs, what an honor. I have long admired you from afar. Bob Meadows. I loved your book. Positively adored it. I've read it six times. Or is it seven? Never mind. Thank you so much for coming."

"The fact that we've remained friends is an indication of how much I value the man," Jacob said.

"Never mind Jacob. He was born with a rampant gene. All behaviorists possess this. It requires them to spend their entire lives hunting madly for order inside the chaos of human existence."

"Bob and I were roommates in college," Jacob said. "We've been arguing ever since."

"And with good reason. When I heard what he'd said to you at the Emory event, Dr. Burroughs, I was mortified. Jacob has always assumed that a good mind and a faculty with words make him right on all matters. It is one of his greatest faults. I hope he has apologized."

"Profusely," Jacob confirmed.

"Please come this way." Bob Meadows started down the carpeted hallway. "My patient is extremely concerned about confidentiality. He'll no doubt insist upon hearing this from your own lips. I've been treating his daughter, who has a substance abuse problem. Then six days ago, he called and requested an appointment of his own."

He knocked on the double-doors of a suite. At a muffled response from within, he opened the doors and said, "Senator, your visitors are here."

United States Senator Mario Suarez was a bullish man. Everything about him was stubby and aggressive, even the way he sat. He crouched on one corner of the seat, as though angry with the need to remain in the chair. He gripped the chair arms hard enough to bunch his shoulders and crease his suit jacket. "I want you to stop these dreams."

"Dreams," Jacob repeated. "Plural."

"Two of them. Bob here tells me the others have also had the second one."

Bob confirmed, "All five of the clinicians we've been in touch with have reported the same."

"This second dream," Jacob said. "Could I confirm, Senator, it follows the pattern of—"

"The street, the crowd, the line, the soup kitchen. Yeah, it's the same." His English was perfect, and harsh in the manner of one used to wielding power. Mario Suarez was a very familiar face, a spokesperson for the Latin-American community, conservative and family-oriented and hardworking and determined to call this country their own. He was Cuban by heritage, and impatient by nature. "I got the message. Now call them off."

Elena had no problem letting the others speak. Jacob glanced her way, noted her determined silence, and said, "It's not that simple, Senator."

Senator Suarez tapped his gold ring on the chair arm. A rapid staccato beat. "What about some kind of pill?"

"We've been through this," Bob Meadows said in his serene voice. "The others who used sleeping aids all found themselves trapped in the dreams. They say it just cycles over and over."

"That can't happen. Once is bad enough." The senator punched the space between him and the window. "You see the mess this country is in right now. I've got a hundred different crises I'm supposed to be dealing with. I can't go into the next finance committee meeting and scream my head off about some dream."

Jacob asked, "What if this is the only way the dreams will stop?"

Elena felt herself confronted by the dreaded prospect and shuddered.

Senator Suarez barked, "Forget it. Not happening."

"Just think about it for a moment," Jacob pressed gently. "Every recipient of these dreams has felt an urgent need to tell the world. What if the dreams stop once you all tell the world—"

"I'll take the dreams." The senator's teeth ground with angry determination. "Look. My grandfather sailed here from Cuba with my father in his arms. My grandmother died in the crossing. I've spent my whole life to get where I am today. I do this for my people. I'm not going to shame myself or them or my grandfather's memory by standing up and making a fool of myself."

Elena had a sudden sense of an unseen portal opening before her. Beyond it was an image of what was coming. What now seemed inevitable. As though everything had been leading up to this point. The recent book tour, the notoriety, her move to Florida, Rachel's arrival, even the meeting with Jacob Rawlings—all of it moving steadily toward this moment.

Jacob said thoughtfully, "What if it only requires one person?"

"A spokesperson," Bob Meadows agreed. "Someone who makes the announcement on behalf of all the dreamers."

Senator Suarez brightened immensely. "Now you're talking."

"This could work," Bob said. "It will need to be someone who can garner this level of attention . . ."

All three men turned her way. Elena saw the door looming up ahead. She knew it was there, and knew she had no choice but to say the words. Even so, she had to claw for the breath to speak.

"I'll do it."

8

The phone call came as they stepped from the elevator into the hotel lobby. Elena reached into her purse. "I'm sorry. I thought I turned this thing off."

"You probably did," Bob Meadows said. "My daughter claims the newest ones have a mind of their own."

"This is Elena."

Rachel Lamprey's voice was brusque to the point of rudeness. "Where are you now?"

"The Ritz-Carlton."

"The one in Coral Gables, yes? I know it. Hold on." The phone went silent.

Jacob asked, "Who is it?"

"The same woman who called as we were leaving Orlando. Her name is Rachel Lamprey."

"She's a patient?"

"No. Rachel is . . ." Elena wondered how to encapsulate Rachel and Miriam and the ancient tomes and all that had gone before.

Bob supplied, "Another dream recipient?"

"No. But she is definitely involved." Elena held up one finger as the phone clicked back to life.

Rachel said, "The company jet will be landing in the Coral Gables private airfield in exactly eighty minutes."

"I drove down in my car."

"A corporate staffer will meet you planeside. Give them the keys. They will drive it back to Melbourne. I will have a car deliver you when we're done here."

"I can drive—"

"This can't wait. Things are happening."

"All right. But how are you able to—" Elena stopped talking because the line went dead.

The hotel shared a small hill with a pair of apartment buildings and a high-rise office complex. The circular brick drive sloped down to join the town's main shopping street. Jacob and Bob Meadows listened carefully to her description of Rachel Lamprey and the mysterious summons, then both men agreed that if the corporation considered it so urgent as to send a private jet, they should probably make themselves available. Bob Meadows suggested they walk down to a shop he knew that did nice takeout meals. There was nothing at the regional airfield but a fuel depot, the offices, and some candy machines.

The two men slipped into the easy companionship of years. They talked as professionals and as friends, going over the meeting with the senator as they had probably discussed hundreds of other cases. They did not exclude Elena. She was given space in their small company, and made welcome. Her silence was simply part of the moment, a trait they accepted because they accepted her.

Elena wished she could share their camaraderie. It would have been so nice to spend an hour or so talking as a clinician in the company of her peers. But the prospect of going public loomed before her. Its huge anxious bulk enveloped her. She felt isolated and alone.

Elena had no idea why she disliked the public spotlight. There had once been a time when she had thought fame would be nice. While she was writing the book, she had often imagined herself standing at the podium and expounding to the world. But once she arrived in that very spot, she had discovered that it was a poisonous light, at least for her.

In her experience, the problem was not the glare of publicity, but rather everything else. All the potential goodness was leeched away by stress and travel and repetitive questions and empty faces. Most of the radio and television interviewers had no idea who she was, or what she had written. They had assistants who read the book and prepared the questions and made all the arrangements. Elena arrived on set, was prepped by these same aides, had her face and hair fashioned into a brittle mask for the cameras, then was ushered into an uncomfortable chair that still smelled from the last guest. The interviewers did not speak to Elena at all. Instead, they played for the camera and the unseen public. Elena was made to feel like a rank amateur, granted a brief moment on this very odd stage, before being whisked off and her place taken by another amateur, everyone competing for a spot in an alien world.

Her public appearances were hardly any better. She was always rushed. The greater her acclaim became, the larger the crowds, the less time she had to speak meaningfully with anyone. She was met planeside by a handler who whisked her from book signing to interview to podium. She arrived at her hotel late and exhausted. She was woken up too early, and forced into another whirlwind day. Over and over, until she saw nothing and felt less.

And now it was all about to happen again.

Elena's sense of disconnect from Jacob and Bob's discussion meant she was the only one who saw the approaching threat.

A figure rode toward them on a motorcycle, one of those machines where they were crouched like jockeys on a racehorse. The driver wore black leather with red lightning bolts on the jacket and the pants. His face was hidden beneath a helmet with a mirrored surface—at least Elena assumed it was a man; she could not be certain. His knee-high boots were drawn up almost to his chest, and he leaned forward to grasp the controls. It was a machine built for speed, and yet the motorcycle crawled down the street. The engine rumbled like a pot about to explode.

It was neither afternoon nor dusk, but rather another of those slow Florida processions toward night. The sun had long since set. But there was no hurry to the close of day. The sky was streaked with a painter's languid brush, as if nature wished to apologize for the storms and the humid heat. Jacob and Bob walked in tandem just ahead of her. Their heads were back, as they softly laughed toward the sky.

The motorcyclist removed one gloved hand from the handlebars and slipped it into the top of his boot. He came out with something black and long. Elena realized this was a silenced gun.

As this was still registering, Elena noticed the white van just ahead of them. A side door was open, and the shadows inside congealed into approaching doom.

"Down! Get down!"

Elena threw herself into the two men. They fell onto the pavement in an astonished heap, landing behind a delivery truck. The silenced guns sounded like a stuttering engine of death.

Elena knew their only hope was to raise the alarm. She had no idea she could scream as loud as she did.

From their position beneath the truck, she could see copper casings fall like lethal rain on the vehicle's other side. Fragments of the building struck her. Sparks flew off the pavement. And still she screamed.

It seemed like eons before the motorcyclist roared away. The van's engine boomed and the tires screeched and suddenly it was over.

Only then did she see the blood oozing from Bob's forehead.

9

⸎ ————————— ⸎

The SuenaMed corporate jet was huge and plush. The three of them piled on board and split up. They had all been enormously shaken by the attack. They needed solitude to reknit the fabric of their existence. They were successful in a profession that was known for its calm facade. They were paid to remain aloof and intact, while all of their patients tumbled into panic and despair. Elena took a seat at the very front of the jet. A walnut burl table stretched before her, with sterling silver cup holders embedded in its polished surface. The pilot's face appeared on the flat screen on the table's other side. He greeted them and described the short flight to Orlando and asked if they needed anything. He seemed accustomed to their terse responses.

Elena shut her eyes to the jet's acceleration down the runway. She allowed the attack to replay behind her eyelids. She saw the sparks and the bullet casings. She felt the rawness of her throat from the screaming. She saw the frightened faces that observed them from doorways up and down the shopping street. She saw Bob and Jacob talk with the police. She heard her own hoarse responses to their questions. She saw her fingers tremble as she pulled out her cell phone to tell Rachel they could not make it to the airport on time, because of needing to go to the police station, then handing the phone to Jacob because it hurt her throat to talk. She felt the trembling of Jacob's own hand as he took it from her.

The plane waited. The pilots might have known why their three passengers arrived ninety minutes late, or perhaps the wary look they gave them was their customary manner of greeting SuenaMed executives.

Elena opened her eyes when Jacob touched her shoulder and asked if she wanted something to drink. Suddenly she was very thirsty. The police had given her a cup of the most awful coffee she had ever tasted. She asked Jacob for a tea with milk and several sugars. He must have heard the raw timbre to her words, for he said he would see if they had any honey.

He returned and set down a china cup and saucer embossed with the SuenaMed logo. He settled into the seat across the aisle. The oversize plush chair was white doeskin leather. Jacob used both hands to hold his own cup. He stared at the blank flat screen on the wall in front of his seat for a time, and then said, "You saved my life."

She watched the faint trembles ripple across the surface of her tea and took a sip. It was warm and sweet and went down easy. She sighed.

"I didn't want to contact you, of course. I felt as though I was dragged kicking and screaming to the only avenue that offered any sense at all to the situation."

Bob Meadows slipped into the chair behind Jacob. He did not speak. He just listened. His face was as white as the butterfly bandage on his forehead, where he had been struck by a flying rock. His wife and children were at their cabin in the North Carolina mountains where he was scheduled to join them the following week. Bob's fear was a palpable force. He did not so much sit in the seat as quiver.

Jacob went on, "Your entire premise rocks my world. The first time I read your book, I was furious. Your perspective on human behavior originates from an entirely different direction. You use dreams as a reason to draw in . . ."

When he stopped, Bob Meadows nudged him in the arm. "You might as well say the word, buddy."

Jacob did not speak.

"God," Bob Meadows said. "The divine hand. The one at work with us this evening. I for one can't stop praying right now. Giving thanks for the chance to draw another breath. Watch my children grow up. Hold my wife . . ."

Elena watched Jacob reach down and touch the lever to unlock his seat. He swiveled around to where he faced her across the aisle. Jacob pretended not to notice as his friend struggled to regain control. He said, "If I insert an invisible force into human behavior, my entire professional world is demolished. By saying that one word. That is why I resented needing to make contact. No matter how great the need. Because . . ."

Bob Meadows's voice was both hoarse and overly deep, as though he had been the one screaming. "Your desire to measure human faculties is not wrong. It is *crucial*. The science of psychology depends upon identifying all components of the human psyche that are quantifiable. The mistake lies in claiming that everything about human life can be measured."

Jacob Rawlings was drawn around against his own will. His gaze looked haunted.

Bob went on, "It is not your professional life that is challenged. That is a mask. It is your *personal* life. It is the way you see yourself. Alone and independent, standing at the pinnacle of your career, beholden to no one. The same internal forces that have kept you single and flitting from one lady to the next are the precise same reasons why you find Elena's perspective so threatening."

Jacob tried his best to offer Elena a mocking smile. "We've been having this same argument since college."

Elena watched the two men and felt an immense rightness to the moment. She sipped from her cup and decided it was time to share what she had been pondering since arriving at the police station. "We're missing something."

Jacob asked, "You mean, about the attack?"

"This plane," Elena replied.

"What about it?"

"How much do you think it costs?"

"A Gulfstream Five, top of the line, looks brand-new." Jacob shrugged. "Twenty, maybe twenty-five. Why?"

Bob Meadows said, "Twenty-five *million*?"

"What did you think, thousand?"

"Man, whose life did you drop in on?"

"The Discovery Channel has three of them. Not as nice, but hey, after a while they're all just another limo with wings." Jacob turned his attention back to Elena. "Go on."

"It's not just the plane. It's everything to do with Rachel Lamprey."

Bob asked, "Who?"

"She's the SuenaMed exec who got us this ride," Jacob said impatiently. "Let the lady finish."

Between sips of her tea, Elena related how she had come to know Rachel, and about the initial contact. The first patient, her own dream, and the mounting pressure Rachel had exerted. "All the while, her company is bearing down on their biggest product launch in decades."

Jacob snapped his fingers. "Sure. SuenaMind. I've been reading about this. It's huge."

Bob asked, "Rachel Lamprey is responsible for SuenaMind?"

"She is the senior product director."

"So what is she doing, working on this dream issue?"

"That is exactly my point." Elena drank again, or started to, then noticed that her cup was empty.

Jacob rose and took it from her. "More honey?"

"Please."

He swiftly returned. "You're saying Rachel Lamprey is behind the attack tonight?"

"I'm saying it's a vital issue. We're all clinicians. We're trained to look in the direction that our patient does not want us to go. See beneath the surface." She paused for a sip. "The attack happened with pinpoint accuracy. They knew about the meeting with the senator. Whom did you tell?"

"Me?" Bob Meadows shook his head. "Not a soul. Not even my secretary. That was part of my arrangement with the senator."

"Jacob?"

"I phoned my office before we left for Miami. I'll miss appointments tomorrow morning. But I didn't tell them about the Ritz."

"The only person I contacted was Rachel. I didn't tell her where precisely we were headed, just that we were driving to Miami for a meeting."

"They could have followed us down," Jacob said.

"Perhaps." Images of the attack flashed through her mind. She set down the cup, her stomach suddenly very queasy. "They were probably waiting for us to emerge with the car, then decided hitting us on the sidewalk was even better."

"But why would Rachel demand you become involved in all this, then set us up for an attack?"

"That," Elena replied, "is the first question I intend to ask."

·   ·   ·

The plane landed at Orlando's second airport, the one closer to downtown. They were met by a limo and a nervous young aide who apologized for Rachel's absence, but she had become tied up in a meeting that would go on for hours more.

The aide drove with them to the Renaissance and saw them checked into a trio of suites. The three of them bid one another a weary good night. Jacob and Bob were busy on their cell phones as they let themselves into their rooms. The next day was Saturday, so Elena had no need to check in with the college. No one waiting for her at home. No one who might worry over where she had been, or was going.

She filled the bath and used the plastic vial of bath oils. The water was spicy and inviting. She felt her muscles gradually relax in the heat. When the water cooled she bundled herself into a fluffy hotel robe and slipped into bed. She could feel the little jerks of tension pull at her muscles. It was unlikely she would sleep well, or for very long. She was glad merely for solitude and safety.

Her questions danced in the dark room. She decided that Rachel Lamprey was not behind the attack. It made no sense to plan an assault and then place the expensive corporate jet at their disposal. Yet Elena sensed that the woman was somehow connected.

Elena's ability to search beyond the unseen had aided her greatly in any number of cases. Then as now, she could not say anything until the evidence was gathered. No patient's treatment could be based on hunches. But the value was still there, for these intuitive thoughts often pointed her in the right direction. And that was what she sensed now.

It all came down to the dreams. And her own next step. The prospect of what awaited her was wrenching.

Elena carried the sense of dread with her into sleep.

·　　·　　·

Saturday morning, a tall man in a dark jacket bearing the Suena-Med logo stood outside Elena's suite when she opened the door. He nodded a silent greeting and watched as she knocked on the men's doors. He accompanied them downstairs and waited while they bought clothes in the hotel's shopping arcade. The only time he spoke was to say that they should charge all of the items to their room.

Breakfast was an elegantly grim affair. The restaurant was jammed. All attention remained fastened on the televisions positioned around the walls. Elena's throat still felt raw, and her words carried a resonant burr. She ate slowly, and the news congealed her breakfast into a viscous lump.

For once, the newscasters had lost their professional brightness. They replayed images from the previous day, when the British financial panic had spread to two other High Street banks. Police had been called out in London, Manchester, Edinburgh, and Birmingham. The lines were forced into angry order. The people inside the banks jammed the counters and crammed their pockets and briefcases and purses with loot. Like they were robbing the place, rather than taking out what was theirs. The prime minister and the Bank of England chief both assured the public and pleaded for calm. No one listened. Bank stocks on Wall Street and London plunged. A red ticker tape below the newscaster relayed data from stock markets in the Far East. Elena did not see the numbers, only how the red ribbon pulled them all closer and closer to oblivion.

A uniformed driver came in and said their car was ready. They left the restaurant and passed through a lobby filled with more silent people and echoes of television news. They rode together in silence.

The SuenaMed headquarters was a gleaming white block set like a crown jewel in the middle of its very own campus. The grounds were beautifully maintained, a velvet display of lawns and flowers and blooming trees. The limo was waved through the main gates and pulled up in front of the entrance, where Reginald opened Elena's door and said, "Rachel is waiting for you upstairs."

They swept through the lobby so fast Elena caught only a fleeting glimpse of backlit photos and awards and elegance. The elevator whooshed them up to the sixteenth floor, three from the top, and opened into a lobby. The receptionist's desk was a curved artwork of blond wood. Reginald snapped his phone shut and greeted Elena with "Perhaps your guests would care to wait here?"

"No," Elena replied. "They would not."

Reginald started to object, then saw something in her face that changed his mind. "This way."

He led them down a short hallway to a corner office, where he knocked and opened and ushered them inside. "Elena has arrived."

Rachel glared at the two men. "Who are they?"

"With me." Elena seated herself. "Dr. Jacob Rawlings, Dr. Bob Meadows, this is Rachel Lamprey."

"We need to talk, Elena. Alone."

"It is not happening. Nothing is, without these two at my side." Elena burned her with a look. *You want tough? No problem.*

"All right. Fine." Rachel planted her elbows on the desk. "Are you finally ready to fulfill your destiny?"

"Not until we get some answers."

"The clock is ticking. The world is waiting. You need—"

"Why is SuenaMed involved? I'm not talking about you. I'm speaking—"

"I know what you mean. And I can't answer your question with strangers present."

"What would you call *me*? We've known each other all of three days."

Rachel's head canted slightly, as though inspecting Elena through a new framework. "The attack must have shaken you more than I thought."

"Thank you for bringing up the attack. I want to know what role SuenaMed played in this. And why you won't answer my question."

Rachel studied the three of them in turn. "Dr. Jacob Rawlings I have at least heard of. This other gentleman . . ."

"Dr. Meadows is a practicing clinician in the Miami area," Jacob replied. "And my closest friend."

Elena added, "And has a patient who has been experiencing the dreams."

"A patient with considerable power on the national stage," Jacob finished.

Rachel rose to her feet. "Wait here."

Rachel returned fifteen minutes later and ushered them up to the top floor. The penthouse was designed as a separate structure, a palace of power and wealth. The ceilings were impossibly high, the sounds muted. The furnishings caught the light and shimmered. People rushed by, their footsteps muffled by the plush carpets, their conversations swallowed by the vast chambers and the hushed air.

Elena found herself distanced from it all. She knew the answers were coming, and they would alter the course of her life. Of this she had no question.

They were brought into a lavish outer office and invited to sit, offered coffee or anything else their hearts might desire. Privacy, Elena wanted to say. A chance to pray and heal and find a clear way forward. But even here, in the elegant silence, she could hear the clock ticking. Out beyond the polarized glass, the world waited for her once again.

Trevor Tenning, CEO of SuenaMed, was everything that old money should be. His hair was silver, his grip solid, his smile perfect. His tan gleamed, his suit fit perfectly. His every gesture carried a smooth sense of his own self worth. He had worn his power so long he considered it his birthright.

Only the shadows beneath his eyes belied the inner turmoil.

He ushered them across the pair of Persian carpets to a sofa set by the corner windows. They looked out over all of Orlando, the tall spires, the emerald forests, the glistening lakes. Rachel seated herself on the sofa beside Trevor. Reginald remained standing.

When they refused his secretary's offer of coffee, Trevor waited until the door to his vast office clicked shut, then said, "Rachel assures me that I can rely on your complete confidentiality."

"Dr. Rawlings and Dr. Meadows are both practicing clinicians, and hold to the same professional oaths as myself," Elena replied. Now that they were this close to answers, she found herself increasingly impatient. "Either you trust us or you don't."

"You are right, of course." He planted his hands on his knees and declared, "I have been having the most dreadful dreams."

Bob Meadows huffed his shock. Jacob exhaled softly. Elena only nodded.

"You do not seem surprised, Dr. Burroughs."

"It is the most logical answer," Elena replied. "Your company is facing a critical juncture. And yet the director of this huge new product's development is given free rein to spend the company's money. On dreams."

"I understand you knew Ms. Lamprey's sister."

"Miriam was my best friend." Elena glanced at the polished woman seated beside the chairman. Rachel belonged here, she decided. Just as much as Miriam had been suited to the sunlit rear porch of her Victorian home on Notting Hill. Elena swallowed a sudden lump of longing for all that once had been, and said to the woman, "I'm surprised you shared this."

The chairman responded, "Rachel and I share a great many things. She and I have been through a number of bruising battles since my arrival here four years ago. She is my right hand, and I would like to think a very dear friend. It is only natural she would share with me about her family."

Rachel spoke for the first time since entering the office. "Trevor knows about Miriam's books."

"Yes indeed. Do you have them?"

"They are locked inside a safety deposit box in London."

"Pity. I would so like to see them."

Rachel said, "You don't think they might be of assistance to us now?"

Elena saw Jacob's frown of confusion and said, "I will explain later." To the pair on the sofa she replied, "I carry images in my computer. The answers we require are not there. At least, not yet. But more importantly, it is not the book at all. But the power *behind* the book."

"You are speaking of your God."

"He is yours too."

Even his nod carried a smooth polish. Even his words, "It would certainly be comforting to know there is a divine hand that is planting these seeds. Perhaps the terror would be easier to bear."

Rachel shifted impatiently on the sofa. "I hate how my sister is winning here."

The chairman turned slowly to her. "Winning?"

"All my life I fought against the clutches of my family. The history. The traditions. The faith. While still at university, I became determined to make a success of my life, on my terms. No one else's. Dreams were part of everything I despised. The obsession. The link to a past where women were enslaved. I am my own person. I have shaped my own personal destiny. Not some invisible deity."

Elena asked, "Do I look enslaved to you?"

"No," Rachel almost spat the word. "Only misguided."

"Then why," Elena asked, "did you come to me?"

Rachel glowered at the onyx table between them and did not speak.

Trevor Tenning cleared his throat. "The real question before us is, what do we do now?"

Elena nodded slowly. She knew the time had come. "You brought me here because you already know the answer."

Bob said, "I don't understand."

Elena found it easier to respond to a fellow clinician. "Trevor Tenning is filled with the same urgent need as me and all the other dreamers. He has to tell the world."

"It is a need that consumes me," Trevor agreed. "At this pivotal point in my company's global operations, I can think of nothing else."

Rachel said, "Now you see."

Elena's motions had grown to where her entire upper body slowly rocked. "But you can't, can you? Not without jeopardizing everything you and your firm have invested. You needed an outsider. Someone who could take the step for you. Someone with recognized authority on the subject of dreams. Someone who would make the world listen."

Trevor Tenning looked at his associate. "You were right all along."

Elena knew they were waiting. She saw the light of comprehension in Jacob's gaze, and wished he would say the words for her. But that was not his role. It was hers. Much as she loathed the prospect. The hour had arrived. Elena said, "It is time to go public."

10

When the meeting with Tenning ended, Rachel rode with them to the floor occupied by the division she ran. As she exited the elevator, Rachel slipped into professional mode. Elena had done it herself often enough. Rachel's tone became crisp, direct. A general issuing orders. "You will have your own suite of offices."

"I don't need—"

"You have no idea what you will need. We haven't even started. There could be a thousand different things that arise. Trevor has placed SuenaMed's resources at your disposal. I would advise you to take full advantage."

Rachel's assistant was there to greet them. Reginald announced, "You have the conference call with Germany and France in two minutes."

"And the press conference?"

"We've scheduled it in an hour and a half."

"Take charge here." She said to Elena, "My PR people are putting together a news conference. We've managed to pull together a solid audience, especially for a Saturday."

She strode off before Elena could formulate an objection. Reginald said, "Shall I get you settled?"

The floor was dominated by the largest open-plan workspace Elena had ever seen. The ceiling was almost warehouse height. Multicolored glass bricks and blooming plants formed borders between the office areas. Illuminated smart boards showed time-lines and ticking clocks on the two sidewalls. Even on a Saturday morning, the atmosphere was quietly frenetic. Most of the faces were young and energetic and so very alive. This floor was clearly Rachel's domain; very efficient, very demanding, yet somehow maintaining a distinctly feminine feel. Elena had a fleeting wish she could tell Miriam what she had found here. How Rachel might be her own person, and very different from her older sister, but still carried traits that were remarkably similar to Elena's departed friend.

Reginald led her to a glass-walled corner office connected to a conference room. He touched one switch to turn on the lights, and another to turn the wall opaque. "The wall is electronically controlled, and also baffles all sound." He turned the walls transparent once more and indicated the adjoining conference room. "I suppose your associates can set up in there."

Bob Meadows cleared his throat. "Actually, I need to be returning to Miami. My office is in a panic. I have a patient who has escaped rehab, and another who may require institutional care."

Elena listened as Reginald made arrangements for him to return home, and dreaded hearing the same farewell from Jacob. But her former nemesis merely stood at the window and frowned over the city beyond.

Bob shook Elena's hand with both of his own, leaned in close, and said, "I will be praying for you. Night and day."

"Thank you."

"A word of advice?"

"Of course."

"Trust Jacob. Beneath all the razor-sharp edges beats the heart of a very caring man."

When they were alone, she joined Jacob by the window. Orlando was a study in contrasts. Skyscrapers dotted the downtown landscape. But the city was blanketed by trees and lawns and lakes. From this height, it appeared to be a well-tended garden where people lived and worked in an almost idyllic setting. The sun shone, the sky gleamed a bright blue, and yet on the horizon lurked a very dark stripe. Elena stared at the approaching thunderstorm and shivered.

Jacob glanced over. "Do you want to talk about it?"

It was a standard opening line, and under any other circumstances would be good for a smile. But today, Elena said, "Out there to the east I have classes. A place at a college that welcomes me. A few new patients." She took a breath. "A life."

Jacob finished for her, "And here in this place, all you have are new responsibilities you don't want."

"But volunteered for," Elena finished. "I feel so conflicted."

"I'm sure you do. And trapped." He frowned at the city below. "I need to go back and see to things at my office. I can return on Monday. If you want me to."

"If I want?"

"I just thought—"

"You just thought what? That I would rather do this alone?"

"No. Of course not." He grimaced. "I suppose I was hoping you would not need me, and I could go back to my—"

"Don't even think such a thing. This is as much your doing as anyone's."

He nodded slow acceptance. "I'll rejoin you after the weekend."

She stared at him. His stony expression only heightened his

good looks. "How many of your young female patients fall in love with you?"

He met her gaze, but did not smile. "Almost as many as the number of male patients whose hearts you steal."

"I'm not a thief."

"And I," he replied, "am not a lecher."

"I never said you were."

"No. That's right. You never attacked me personally. You never questioned my character or my motives." He turned back to the glass wall overlooking Orlando. "It was one of the things I most admired about you. Even when I most despised your work."

She turned with him, looking out over the emerald-green city. "I can't believe I'm actually seeking your advice."

He was silent for a long moment, then said, "Going public with this could be an act of professional self-destruction."

"Worse than my book on dreams?"

"That was a questionable piece of research. This is a public pronouncement of impending doom. You are going to be overwhelmed by the bizarre fringe elements."

Elena lowered her head. "I feel as though my life has been ripped from my control. Again."

He settled a hand upon her shoulder. The act of a friend offering strength. She fought against a sudden tide of tears. If he noticed, he did not say. Instead, he asked, "You want me, your nemesis, to tell you not to do this?"

"Yes," Elena replied. "Please."

"I wish I could," Jacob said. "So much. But I can't."

Rachel came for her an hour later. "We're ready."

Elena turned to where Jacob still stood by the window. He was watching her now, his back to the world outside, his gaze haunted by myriad things she could not fathom. Elena turned in a slow circle, looking for a reason not to go forward with this, a way out. Reginald stood behind Rachel, filling the only doorway. Elena stood inside an elegant glass cage. Trapped.

Rachel crossed the room and picked up the controls to the flat screen from the shelf behind the empty desk. She turned it to MSNBC, and kept her hand out, using the control to point at the screen. "Look."

"No, I don't—"

"*Look.*" Rachel turned up the sound just as the pretty business newscaster said, "Off-hour trading shows markets down around the globe. I'm joined now by the chief broker with Bank of America's London branch. Glenn, what's happening over there?"

"If this wasn't a Saturday, I'd call it a crash." The man sounded as though he had breakfasted on gravel. "I dread to think what's going to happen on Monday."

Behind the broker, the bank's trading floor was one degree off pandemonium. The camera panned a giant room filled with screaming, gesticulating people. The newscaster asked, "Can you tell me what is behind the panic?"

"The London bank run caught us off guard. Now we're hearing rumors about more disasters to come. Dublin, Rome, Athens. Take your pick. Nobody can track down what's real. You're seeing the herd mentality at its worst."

"What do you see as the next logical step?"

"Logical? Did you really use that word?" His laugh carried a manic edge.

Rachel cut off the television and stepped in close enough for Elena to smell her perfume. The scent was subtle, expensive, and suited the woman perfectly. "You must do this," Rachel said softly. "You must do this *now*."

. . . .

The news conference was a dread event.

Rachel and Reginald and a chirpy young PR specialist led her onto the stage. The podium was glass and set to one side of a gigantic screen. Two more screens filled the edges of the stage. Only when Elena was seated did she realize her face would soon be up there on display.

Rachel walked to the podium and introduced herself. Without preamble, she said, "Something has come to our attention that could well have repercussions far beyond the scope of SuenaMed's current research and product lines. I wish you to know that everything you hear has the backing of our CEO, Trevor Tenning, and the board of directors."

The room was not full. Perhaps fifty men and women were seated in the steeply banked seats rising up to where a trio of television cameras was focused on the stage. Some journalists sat at the ready, notebooks out and pens tapping the empty page. Others sprawled in the haphazard manner of people who would prefer to be somewhere else. A couple had iPads hooked up with one earphone in place, listening to Rachel with one ear while watching news feeds.

Rachel said into her mike, "Patch us into MSNBC."

The trio of screens came to life with blaring intensity. The same images Elena had seen upstairs assaulted the audience. Journalists sat up straighter, exchanged glances, pulled out their earphones.

Elena lowered her head and offered up a brief prayer. She had a dozen different wishes, most of them desperate. But the only words that came to her with utter clarity were, *Be with me.*

Rachel had to raise her voice to be heard. "Cut the sound." When the room went silent, she went on, "What you are about to hear may sound out of place in this day and age. But I repeat what I said at the beginning. SuenaMed's senior executives have given this careful study. We concur that what is happening is real, and vital. I would now like to introduce Dr. Elena Burroughs, a respected psychologist and clinician. Some of you may know her as a specialist on dream analysis, and author of the international bestseller, *The Book of Dreams*. Dr. Burroughs?"

If God was in this moment, Elena could not detect him. She felt no guidance as she approached the podium, nor any sense of genuine peace. Instead, there was only the moment, only the looks of skepticism that confronted her. So she responded as she would to approaching colleagues with information they would prefer to dismiss. With clinical detachment.

"From the analytical perspective, dreams fall into three basic categories. The first are commonplace, and form a backdrop upon which the subconscious can work through the dreamer's waking life. The second category includes all attempts by this same subconscious to deal with deeper issues, core fears, and severe traumas."

The room was filled with the buzzing of barely muffled conversation. She saw a few smirks, a few head shakes, some unmistakable gestures. Elena grimly continued, "The third category is the most disputed. And has to do with dreams of foretelling."

A pair of younger men toward the back of the room laughed out loud. The room took this as a signal to raise the volume. Elena let it continue for a moment, then rapped her knuckles on the Plexiglas podium. "I must ask that you please be quiet." When this did not work, she motioned to Reginald, who rose from his seat. Elena said, "Anyone who finds it difficult to grant me the chance to conclude my remarks will be evicted."

There was a shocked quality to the stillness. No matter how powerful the figure, most business executives feared the press and their ability to destroy. Elena could not have cared less. "At its most basic, foretelling is controversial because it defies the logic of our daily existence. It suggests that the dreamer has the ability to pierce time and distance and human limits.

"The reason I have been asked to speak with you today is because we have evidence that just such a dream of foretelling has been occurring. Now. Today. By a number of individuals who have no physical connection. They do not know each other. They have never met. And yet, they all share the same images."

This time, the silence was genuine. A voice spoke directly in front of her. "Does this mean different people are having similar dreams?"

"I would ask that you raise your hand and be recognized before speaking. To answer your question, no, that is not what I mean at all. These subjects are not having similar dreams. They are *exactly* the same. They follow a *precise* pattern. One that defies any form of standard analysis." A hand rose toward the back. "Yes."

"What are the dreams about?"

"The current financial crisis." Now it appeared that every hand in the room shot up. She pointed at another. "You by the aisle."

"How many of these dreamers are there?"

"Eleven. They stretch right around the globe. They come from a variety of economic strata. They include senior politicians and international business leaders. They share only one thing. All of them have experienced the same two dreams."

"*Two* dreams?"

"Yes. First one, then the other."

"What are they?"

Elena found it increasingly easy to maintain her clinical tone as she described the two dreams. She concluded with the pressure that all the dreamers felt, the desperate need to warn the world. Then she stopped.

Someone asked, "What's the tie-in to SuenaMed?"

Rachel stepped over to the podium. "That question will be answered at a later date."

The question Elena dreaded finally came from a heavyset woman in a rumpled dark suit. "Am I missing something? What's the story? I mean, the crisis has already happened. Even if they were experiencing what you called it, foretelling, the thing is already foretold."

Elena felt the burning need rise up inside her, an intensity so powerful she gripped the podium with both hands, just to maintain a steady tone. "The dreams are not about what has happened up to this point. They are about what is coming next." Her swallow was audible over the microphones. "If the dreamers are correct, this crisis has not even gotten started."

11

Elena left Orlando in her SUV, which had been brought back from Miami and left in the SuenaMed garage. Rachel had offered to have a company limo drive her back to Melbourne. Elena replied that she had no interest in being driven anywhere else. By anyone. She just wanted to be home.

The drive from SuenaMed's headquarters on the eastern side of downtown Orlando to her home in Melbourne would take her just over an hour. The Beachline Expressway cut a straight swath through the wetlands surrounding the Saint John River. The Jeep Cherokee was bigger than any car she had ever owned. It suited Florida driving. She liked being up high, able to see over most traffic and survey the road ahead. And the easy switch to four-wheel drive meant extra traction was available when required. Like now.

A thunderstorm struck when she was about thirty miles from home. Rain lashed her windshield. Elena switched the wipers to high, but the rain defied their rapid drumbeat. Water draped a translucent curtain over the glass and the noise drowned out her radio. Elena focused on the taillights of the car directly ahead. She told herself to relax. It was just another September storm.

In a brilliant flash of lightning, everything changed.

There was a low roar, a whooshing noise like a freight train bearing down on her. Where before the rain had descended straight down, now it came at her from all sides. She could see nothing.

Then a set of brake lights flashed past her. The car was to her *right*. Off the highway. And moving *backward*.

Elena hit the flashers and pulled onto the verge. For a heart-stopping moment, the car just floated. The brakes instantly started the ABS stuttering. The tires gripped with a jarring that tumbled her against the door. Elena continued off the highway verge and into the grass. She felt the slick bumping and then the ABS kicked in a second time, finally bringing her to a halt.

Elena would not have thought it possible, but the rain intensified. The wind accelerated to a shriek. The downpour struck with such force it pounded her SUV like a metal drum. She covered her ears, trying to clear her head enough to decide what to do.

Then it was over.

The rain and the wind departed as swiftly as they had arrived. Elena's wipers still whipped at a frantic pace, only now they shuddered over dry glass. She cut them off and rose unsteadily from her car.

To the west, the sky over Orlando was a mottled purplish black. The storm rumbled and growled like a hungry predator.

All around her, cars were scattered like children's toys. They faced every direction. One truck had jackknifed across the central grassy strip. As she watched, the driver pushed open his door and slipped to the ground on unsteady legs. He surveyed the scene and crossed himself.

An elderly gentleman struggled from his motor home,

which was pointed back in the direction he had come from. His voice shook as he asked Elena, "What was that?"

"A tornado."

"Glory be." He patted himself. "I've entered the belly of the beast and come out alive."

Elena heard weeping, and stumbled to the minivan behind her. The young woman had both hands locked on the wheel. Her vehicle had spun ninety degrees and faced away from the highway. The young woman stared out the windshield at the marsh beyond the highway fence. Elena called through the glass, "Are you all right?"

The woman stared at her. "Do I *look* all right?"

Elena motioned for her to roll down the window. The woman struggled with the controls. When the window opened, Elena said, "I meant, are you hurt?"

"I . . . No. Yes. I don't . . ." She retook her two-fisted grip on the wheel, and rocked her upper body. "Why is this *happening* to me?"

Elena reached through the window and took hold of the woman's rigid shoulder. She glanced about, saw that the minivan was empty.

"I'm coming back from a job interview. There were *ninety* applicants. The man told me I was lucky to be interviewed. I don't need an *interview.* I need a *job.* We need the *money.* My husband lost his job at NASA. We have kids in school. And now . . ."

"You are just driving home," Elena said, hurting for her. "And you get caught by a tornado."

"I want my life back under *control.*" She released one hand so as to beat against the wheel in time to her words. "I want to feel *safe.* I want to take care of my *family.*"

Elena stood on the wet grass and watched as the cars began to filter back onto the highway. The truck straightened slowly, rumbled across the grass, and gradually accelerated away. Elena asked, "Would you like to pray with me?"

When the woman nodded, Elena spoke words she scarcely heard. After the amen, Elena said, "I am a clinical psychologist. If you think it might help you to talk with someone, I would be happy to meet."

She wiped her eyes. "We can't afford . . . My husband's medical insurance is running out next month."

"There is no question of payment. Do you have a pen and paper?" Elena wrote down her details, handed it back, then asked, "Do you belong to a church?"

"Not for years."

"Perhaps you should think about joining. Most of them will have support groups for families facing situations just like yours. I have found great comfort in worshipping among the family of believers."

The woman put the minivan into gear and said through the open window, "You are an angel from God."

Elena stood there a long moment after the woman drove away. Then she headed home.

Elena sat on her little screened-in porch and cradled the phone in her lap. Out beyond the still waters, lightning flickered from a massive dark wall. She took a long breath and dialed. When Reed Thompson answered, she said the words she had rehearsed a dozen times in her head. "This is Elena Burroughs. I apologize for calling on a Saturday evening, but I am taking you at your word. I am phoning in an hour of need."

"Wait just a moment." There was a muffled conversation, then the president of Atlantic Christian said, "My daughter is taking over the grill. I saw you on the news. Where are you?"

"I've just gotten home."

"Have you eaten?"

"I don't . . . No."

"Come straight over. Please. I insist. We're the pale-brick house just off the entrance to the college. Say, twenty minutes? Excellent. Until then."

Elena dressed hurriedly and left her condo. She did not want to be out in the car again. Especially when it started raining, and lightning rumbled, and the streets grew slick once more. She felt a sudden fear rise up, but pushed it aside. Soon enough she passed through the tall brick gates marking the entrance to ACU. The president's house was just on the right, set back behind a wide oval drive.

Reed had the door open before she cut the motor. He called to her as she rushed through the drizzle, "We just managed to get the grill under the awning before the deluge. Dinner was saved."

"I'm sorry to have bothered—"

"We'll hear no more about that. I'm glad you called. Now give me your coat."

The home was graceful in a professional manner. The president's role included fund-raising, which meant he entertained on a regular basis. It had been this way at Oxford, and was the same here. The president's home was a place for important meetings in a comfortable and elegant setting. It came with the job. A pair of large living rooms opened to either side of the foyer. Behind one was his office, behind the other a formal dining room that could hold twenty people. The kitchen was large enough to support a staff, but tonight it held an informal gathering of family and friends. Reed Thompson introduced the pastor of Riverside Baptist Church, the pastor's wife, and their three sons. There was Gary Jamison, the provost, and the head of the engineering department, a bullish man with a wife who looked like the model she previously had been.

Then a young teenager entered through the rear doors, and Reed introduced his daughter, Stacy. In this willowy young woman, Elena saw traces of the mother who was no more, and whom Elena wished she could have met. Stacy's gaze was happy, her laughter genuine, but the hint of loss was there. She had her father's broad mouth and wide forehead. But the flashing green eyes that captivated all three of the pastor's boys were definitely from the absent mother. As was the hair, the color of mahogany, with streaks of honeyed sunlight.

They dined in a screened alcove off the home's rear. The garden was lit by spots buried by the trunks of a dozen palms. Candles burned from tall metal pillars to either side of the glass table. At the table's center, lilies floated in a crystal bowl. Elena watched the fifteen-year-old Stacy take her mother's place, and imagined the memories that welled up each time she set this table, or lit the candles, or heard in her father's compliments the silent yearning for a woman who had left them too soon.

Over dinner Elena described the tornado. They listened in silence, and replied with genuine concern. Elena then went quiet, and listened as the talk turned to recollections from other hurricane seasons. What she heard was a current that ran far deeper than the spoken words. Here were people she could trust, she decided. Either she opened up, or she didn't. They would not pry. But as she listened to the talk and the quiet laughter, there in the ruddy glow of flickering candles, she saw the faces of friends she had yet to truly know.

She said softly, "I would like to share something with you, and ask your advice."

She talked them through it all. The dreams and the dreamers. And because of the role he played, she told them of Jacob Rawlings. The provost's wife knew him from the television, and called him both handsome and charming. Which, of course, he was. Reed frowned at this, which for some reason caused his observant daughter to smile. When attention turned back to Elena, she went on to describe the assembly of journalists, and the way it had left her feeling.

"The local news channel covered it," Reed Thompson told her. "It's also been picked up by the business cables. I thought you handled yourself very well."

The provost asked, "So you think this is only the beginning?"

"I can only tell you what the dreams have been saying."

"So we could be looking at a new depression."

"Or worse," Reed said. "If it's true."

Only the pastor had not spoken. He was a tall man and held himself slightly stooped. His name was John Daniels. His three sons could have been cloned from the father, dark of hair, with sharp intelligence in their coal-black eyes, all of them even possessing the father's cleft chin. They glanced his way several times, and took note of their father's careful wariness, and said nothing as well. It was Stacy who asked, "Do you think God is behind this?"

The former model said, "How could it be anything else?"

"A dozen people dreaming the same dream around the globe," the provost said. "I'd call that pretty concrete evidence."

Reed asked, "Elena?"

She replied, "This entire year has been very difficult for me. My house in Oxford burned down; my insurance company has claimed criminal actions and refused to pay until the courts decide who is to blame. Almost everything I owned was tied up in my former home. I agreed to a lecture tour, which brought in some income but forced me back into the limelight, which I loathe. I came here, basically wanting to hide away. What happens, but I'm suddenly thrown back onto the stage, and if what I said today is true, this is only the beginning. And all I've been thinking about is how much I dislike this, how distant God seems, how nothing is the way I want it.

"Then after the storm passed I helped a woman on the highway. She was coming back from applying for a job she didn't get.

And I saw another person whose life is out of control. And I finally realized that this isn't about me at all. I need to do God's will. He's taken me out of my comfort zone before, and it wasn't easy, but when it was done I had the feeling . . ."

When Elena hesitated, the pastor spoke for the first time. "Tell us."

"I lost my husband seven years ago. For the longest while, I felt as though life was only going to be half-lived. But in the midst of the turmoil last year, I grew into a new life. It might not have been what I wanted, or how I saw myself. But I had a sense that every day mattered. I'm sorry, I haven't said that at all well."

"You found a new purpose, a new definition of what mattered most." Reed Thompson's voice was low and melodious, as though reading off of a script he had studied for years. "You grew beyond where you had been. You often did not like it, because it meant leaving behind many things you cherished. Or so you thought. But you haven't left anything behind. Have you?"

"No," she murmured. "Not really."

The provost asked, "So what now?"

"I've been rushing around, handling things. Being the professional. And the result is just like those cars on the highway. Twisted in every direction, out of control, no one knowing what just happened or what's coming next. And that's wrong. If I am really here for a purpose, I shouldn't do anything until I have a clear understanding of what God wants from me."

The provost's wife said, "But the dreams."

"The *urgency*," the provost agreed.

"Precisely because this is so important, I must take care," Elena replied. "And right now, all I can tell you is, God has never felt more silent."

The pastor's wife reached out in both directions. "Let's join hands and pray. Elena's right. It's not enough to have dreams. There also has to be *vision*."

12

Reed Thompson and his daughter picked her up for church the next morning. Elena did not want to go. She had woken early from yet another dream, and the burden of dread filled her still. Twice she picked up the phone, intending to call and say that she was unwell. Which was certainly true. But something stopped her, and when the university president's Buick pulled up into her complex's parking lot, she was waiting on the tiny lawn fronting her building.

Reed and Stacy seemed to sense her need for space, and said little on the drive. Elena found the silent car a comfort. The two of them seemed more than daughter and father. They were also friends, people whose relationship had been forged by unwelcome fires, and strengthened as a result. Elena waited until they emerged from the car and Reed was drawn into a conversation to say, "I apologize for being so quiet."

Stacy Thompson held herself with a model's precision, as though aware of her every move, and gesture. This was no doubt the result of serving as her father's partner at any number of public events. Her strong features were accented by a distinctly

Florida tan. She seemed very comfortable within her own skin, which was borne out by her response, "I know all about the need for space, Dr. Burroughs."

"Please, call me Elena."

"When you were walking toward the car, Daddy said you looked like you were being chased by shadows."

"I had a bad night," Elena confessed.

"Was it the dreams?"

She hesitated, then replied, "I've had another one."

"It must be awful, coming under attack when you're most defenseless."

Elena examined the young woman, and decided that was precisely how she would have described the loss of a mother while still a child. "I hadn't thought of it like that. But that is exactly how it feels."

"Here comes Daddy." Stacy Thompson had a great deal of experience at hiding her thoughts behind a professional smile. "I'm glad you came today."

As soon as she entered the Sunday school class, Elena felt the same. The church was a bastion of old Florida, built in the late sixties when the space race was just starting, and Melbourne became home to industries servicing the Cape. It anchored the point where the causeway bridge entered the barrier island. The low whitewashed structures were connected by covered walkways and well-tended tropical gardens. Palms fronted the inland waterway and lined the parking areas. There was an air of calm simplicity to the place, a haven that welcomed and comforted.

Stacy left for the young people's class. Reed Thompson led Elena into a room whose door held a handwritten sign claiming it was for married couples. He introduced her around, then invited everyone to be seated and led the class in an opening prayer. They were studying the second chapter of Daniel.

Reed revealed a different side here, an unexpectedly easygoing nature. He gave a ten-minute review of the passage they had read that week, which involved King Nebuchadnezzar's first dream, and his threat to kill the wise men of Babylon if they could not reveal the message. Then Reed opened the class to discussion.

The class responded with a variety of issues that covered everything from the current economic crisis to problems with children. From time to time, Reed pointed out lessons that could be drawn from that week's Bible passage. Otherwise he let the class take the discussion wherever they wished. The result was part Bible study, part encounter group. Elena observed the people and heard the discussion and decided this was what she needed, a space to reflect in prayer-filled safety.

As they emerged from the church service, Reed Thompson was drawn into a clutch of somber-looking people. Stacy walked over and said, "They're part of the church's governing body. They want Daddy to join. He's said no three times. They think if they keep pestering him he'll change his mind."

"I can understand why they'd want him."

Stacy's gaze was clear and very direct. "You look much better than when we picked you up."

"The time here has helped a great deal."

"I'm glad. Daddy says sometimes the people in there thank him, when all he did was sit and listen."

"Your father," Elena said, "is a remarkable man."

Stacy tilted her head to one side and smiled. "He likes you."

"Excuse me?"

"Last night after you left, Daddy asked me what I thought of you. He never does that."

She found herself wanting very much to know: "What did you tell him?"

"That you're not like Mom. And I think that's a good thing."

"What do you mean?"

"Mom's life focused on the family. At least, that's what I remember. I was only ten when she died. She stopped working when Rob was born. That's my older brother. Rob doesn't like talking about her. But he goes quiet sometimes when he's home, and I know he's thinking about her."

"You are a very perceptive young lady," Elena said.

"For my age," Stacy finished for her.

"Actually, for any age." She hesitated, then added, "But you didn't really answer your father's question."

"That's exactly what Daddy said." Stacy's smile was broader this time. "I told him I'd like to be your friend."

Which was why, when Reed turned around, he found Elena's arm draped around his daughter's shoulders. He took that in, and said merely, "Well, well."

Elena refused their invitation to join them for lunch. Not because she didn't want to go. But because her time away from the world and its demands was over. She told them that, certain that they would understand, and they did. Reed and his daughter both responded with the grave nods of people who had come to know the dictates of a world that only knew one speed—full-bore.

She ate a salad standing at her breakfast counter. Only when she was done with lunch and had brewed a fresh pot of coffee did she turn on her phone. There were a dozen messages, hardly a surprise, given her assumption that the third dream would not have come to her alone. Three of the messages were from Jacob, and she called him first.

He greeted her with "What took you so long?"

"I was at church." She disliked his tone enough to add, "You should try it sometime."

He was silent a moment, then, "Hold on, I want to bring in Rachel. She is as desperate to talk with you as I am."

She heard the phone click back on and Jacob said, "Rachel, can you hear us?"

"Yes. Elena?"

"I'm here."

"Jacob, did you tell her?"

"I wanted to wait until you were with us."

Rachel said, "There's been a third dream."

Jacob said, "We've had it confirmed now by nine of the subjects."

"Don't call them that," Elena said.

"The . . . Why not?"

"They're not subjects. *I'm* certainly not."

"It was just a word," Rachel said.

"It is far more than that. It is a classification, and it is a false one. This is not an experiment. And they are not subjects under anyone else's control."

Her tone forced them both to pause. Jacob said, "How do you want us to refer to them?"

"Call them what they are. Dreamers."

Rachel asked, "Can we please return to the matter at hand?"

"I have never left it," Elena replied.

Rachel said, "You've had the dream also. Haven't you?"

"Yes."

Jacob's tone grew increasingly uncertain. "Yours was the same as the others?"

"Another warning," Elena said. And instantly the images were there in her mind. Filling her interior vision with such brutal force that the world beyond her eyes paled to insignificance. "I stood with a crowd before a window. On the other side, television screens showed markets around the world in a panic. A ticker tape ran across the bottom of the screen. Portugal had defaulted on its national debt."

Jacob said, "This is a definable issue. Portugal has made no such claim."

"We need to go public immediately," Rachel agreed.

"If this announcement is made and then the Portuguese government does as the dream predicts," Jacob said, "we have concrete, definable proof."

Elena waited until she was sure both were done, then asked, "Where do the dreams come from?"

Jacob seemed genuinely confused by her question. "What does that have to do with anything?"

"It is a vital issue. It is also something both of you are doing your best to avoid looking at. What is the dreams' source?"

Rachel demanded, "You want me to say this is God at work?"

"I want you to *confront the question*. I can't tell you what your answer should be. But the subject needs to be addressed."

"You can't imagine what you're asking." Rachel's voice carried a rough anger. "You have no idea."

"I knew Miriam. I know your family's past," Elena replied. "Rachel, we are talking about piercing the veil of time and looking beyond. This is not humanly possible. What does this leave us with?"

When the response was a tense silence, Jacob said, "The question has kept me up all night. My patient called me at one in the morning with this latest dream. Two of the other clinicians called before dawn. Between that first call and the others, I did not sleep. I was too busy wrestling with this very issue."

"And?"

"And I don't know. But I agree, there is at least the possibility that you are right. That some divine power is at work, and we need to acknowledge this."

Elena gave that a moment, wanting Rachel to insert herself. But when Rachel responded, it was to ask, "Are you suggesting this isn't a real crisis? That there's something even bigger going on?"

"I'm saying I don't know. Because God hasn't spoken to me. Or, as far as I can tell, to anyone else involved here."

Jacob said slowly, "If we ask for God's interpreter to come forward, we'll be the laughingstock of the entire world."

"Daniel went before the king, who had pledged to kill anyone who gave the wrong message. He faced certain death, and yet he did as he was told." Elena had never felt more sure of anything in her entire life. "If God intends for us to receive a message, he will make it known in an unmistakable fashion."

"So, you're saying we shouldn't go public?"

"No," Elena replied. "I'm saying we shouldn't pretend to know more than we do. Or take on a greater role than God gives us."

Elena went down to the condo's health club to work out. She would have preferred to go for a run, but the sky was turning black again and she did not want to be caught out. Plus there was the ragged-edged memory of the attack in Miami. She felt safe here inside the gates, with the security guard on constant duty. Out there, running in the open, was a risk she was not ready to take.

As she left her condo and crossed the central grounds, the air was thick and close with coming rain. Elena surprised herself by how little the Florida weather bothered her. After nine cool English summers, she would have expected to wilt like a hothouse rose. But she loved the violent showers, at least when she wasn't caught behind the wheel. The sunsets were a daily display that stopped traffic. Even the hurricane growing beyond the Antilles sparked her daily routine.

Her phone rang just as she reentered the condominium. She checked the readout and answered with "Yes, Jacob."

"Is everything all right?"

"Everything is fine. I just got back from my complex's gym."

"Oh. Well." He cleared his throat. "Rachel and I have talked. She wants to set up a different sort of press conference for tomorrow. We can use their comm link to bring all the dreamers at once. And have them together describe this latest warning."

"Some of them won't want to disclose their identities."

"We've discussed this. We will explain the intention, and give them the choice. Those who want to remain anonymous can keep their cameras blocked."

Jacob hesitated then, so Elena finished for him. "Rachel wants me to officiate."

"We both do. Yes."

"And she doesn't want me to mention God."

"She wants to maintain a professional balance. But we both feel we need someone to address the dreams with the national recognition and authority that you bring."

Elena wondered how Daniel would have handled such a request. Or Isaiah. She said a quick prayer, then said, "All right. When does she want this to take place?"

"Tomorrow morning at eight. Before the New York markets open."

"I'll be there."

After dinner, Elena was watching the evening news when the phone rang. She waited until the worried newscaster had described the world's fearful wait for the markets to reopen Monday morning, then answered, "Hello?"

Vicki Ferrell, her editor, said, "I couldn't wait another minute to hear if the lizard had shed his skin."

"So much has happened," Elena said.

"Tell me about it. Is that the news I hear?"

Elena cut off the television. "Yes."

"Does the handsome Dr. Rawlings play a role in whatever is going on down there?"

Elena rose from the sofa and carried the phone out to the balcony. Beyond the screen and the buzzing insects, the dusk-clad waters rippled softly against the moored boats.

"Elena, are you there?"

"I was just wondering," Elena replied, "whether I should tell you."

"Is this some kind of joke?"

"No, Vicki. No joke."

"I'm your editor. Of course you should tell me. You have to tell me everything. It's in your contract. If it isn't, it should be."

So Elena did. Starting with the first dream and moving through the entire process. To the final dream, the issue of where the dreams originated, the planned newscast.

When she finished, Vicki was silent a moment, then said, "I can't believe I missed your press conference. Why didn't you tell me?"

"This doesn't have anything to do with—"

"With what? Your book? Your career? Girl, get real."

Elena had no idea how to respond, so she remained silent.

"I hope you're taking careful notes. Because when this is over, you are going to write me a new megahit."

"Good night, Vicki."

"And have them make you copies of all your press conferences from now on. I'm serious, Elena. My nose is itching. And I've got the best nose for a hit in the city. Ask anybody."

13

When Elena emerged from her condo early the next morning, she noticed a tall man strolling past the guard station. The road beyond her complex connected with a boatyard and the Merritt Island drawbridge. He could have been going anywhere. But the man looked oddly familiar, as though Elena had glimpsed him before. As she drove through the gates, she stopped and searched in every direction. But the man was nowhere to be seen.

The SuenaMed guards must have been instructed to announce her arrival, because Rachel Lamprey emerged from the elevators before Elena had received her visitor's badge. "Thank you for coming."

"I'm still not sure it's the right thing."

"It is." Rachel's firm response brooked no argument. "Jacob phoned to say his plane was late. I've sent a car to collect him. They're still setting up for the conference. We have a few minutes; why don't we grab a coffee."

The executive dining facilities overlooked an interior garden. A pair of fountains played over bronze sculptures fashioned from the company's name and logo. Directors gathered at other tables paused their discussions to inspect them. Elena felt as though her body vibrated to an unwanted frequency. The last thing she needed was for coffee to further jangle her nerves. She took tea and toast and hoped she would be able to keep them down.

Rachel seated herself at the table's opposite side. She was dressed in a suit of knitted gray silk. "I'm glad you're here. You bring a level of professionalism to this entire process."

"You're the one who looks the professional. You could take center position as well as me. Or better."

"I look like what I am: a senior corporate executive," Rachel said. "Anyone who saw me up there would look for ulterior motives."

Elena sipped her tea, picked up the toast, but decided it would just sit in her stomach like a stone. "I'm wondering the same thing."

Rachel had the same strong features as her departed sister, Miriam. Elena's former friend had spiced her every word with traces of her Middle Eastern heritage. Rachel's diction was perfect, her every word calculated. Only the intelligent dark eyes and the elegant poise spoke of a heritage from beyond these shores. "My motives are simple enough. Trevor Tenning, Suena-Med's CEO, is both my mentor and my close personal friend. Trevor is like a lot of people at the top. He has few people he can trust with the worst. He cannot afford to look vulnerable."

"Or insane," Elena added.

"I might have wondered about that," Rachel confessed. "Had our clinical test subject not reported the very same dream."

"Speaking of which, have you found him?"

Her expression turned intensely grave. "No, and his absence haunts my nights. I can't help but fear that our drug or my interview might have somehow played a role in this."

"I'd say that was unlikely, given how he's the only SuenaMed test case who has had such experiences." Elena hesitated, then added, "I think Miriam would agree."

"How can you say such a thing? Miriam never approved of any decision I made or any action I took."

Elena met the flashing dark gaze straight on. "She would of this. She was very loyal to her friends, and respected this in others. She called it one of the few opportunities most people were given to ever step beyond their own self-interests and serve a higher cause."

Rachel blinked fiercely. "I positively loathed everything to do with Miriam's fixation on dreams."

"It was not a fixation," Elena retorted. "And dreams were not the central point. Not at all."

"When Trevor came to me with this problem, I almost told him to go somewhere else. I wanted to put him in contact with you and wash my hands of the whole affair."

"You did the right thing," Elena said. "Trevor is lucky to have you as a friend."

"I have spent my entire life charting my own course, fighting against my family's heritage. You cannot imagine how women were treated in my culture."

Elena decided to change the subject. "How is your daughter? I'm sorry, I don't remember her name; I only met her that one time at Miriam's funeral."

"Penelope lives in New York. She's been there about a year, ever since her boyfriend gave up acting and they moved back from LA. We talk. Not enough. I try to see her when I am in town. Things with Penny are . . . difficult."

"And your husband?"

"Ex. Boston. Surgeon. Teaches at BU. He's as worried about Penny and her aimless existence as I am. Can we talk about something else?"

"Of course." Elena leaned across the table and asked softly, "Are you having me watched?"

"What?"

"I keep seeing people who look vaguely familiar. Last night there was a pair of fishermen moored near my condo. I thought I'd seen one of them walking around the university campus. Then this morning I recognized a man strolling past my condo's front gates. I think he was the other man on that boat."

Rachel flushed. "I specifically ordered them to stay out of sight. I hired that agency because they are supposed to be discreet."

"They are. For the most part. Why didn't you tell me?"

"I was worried that you would order me to stop. But I can't just allow you to go around unprotected. Not after that attack in Miami. Trevor agrees. We're responsible for getting you involved."

"Is Jacob also being protected?"

"Well, yes. Are you going to tell him?"

"I think one of us should."

"You do it, then."

"All right." Elena studied the woman across the table from her. Everything about Rachel was in carefully refined order. "Why are you doing this? I don't mean helping your friend. I mean doing so publicly."

She responded with customary irritation. "Isn't that obvious? Besides the fact that my mentor and friend asked me, I'm in the business of *healing*. The world is *sick*. If there is a chance I can do *anything* to avert this crisis, I will. Even if it means—"

"Losing control of your own personal situation," Elena finished for her. Elena decided she would probably never be this woman's friend. She doubted Rachel had many real friends. But she could most certainly work with her. "I understand."

"I . . ." Rachel stopped because Reginald Pierce's shadow fell upon the table.

Reginald smiled a greeting to Elena, then said, "It's time."

When the makeup lady finished with Elena's face and hair, Elena was ushered back into the same lecture hall they had used the previous time. Only now the rows of padded folding chairs were almost all occupied. The rear of the room was jammed with television lights and cameras and sound equipment. The press observed her entrance with a cynical eye and talked loudly among themselves. A sound technician fitted her with a microphone and transmitter, then led her onstage.

The crystal podium had been moved to one side. Opposite it was a narrow table covered by a white cloth, fronting two leather chairs. Jacob Rawlings had swiveled his around so a makeup lady could powder his face. He winced a welcome at Elena and said, "They want me to join you."

"I think it's an excellent idea."

"I wish I shared your confidence."

"You are known as a skeptic. Your presence will mean a lot." Elena settled into the chair beside him. "Not to mention steady my nerves."

The drapes behind the stage had been drawn back to reveal a wall of flat screens. Five of the oversize monitors showed faces. The others held a bright blue backdrop with a city and country written in white script. Elena counted the screens and said, "Fifteen dreamers, counting me and Tenning?"

"Four more have been confirmed over the weekend. I have personally checked them out."

"They've all had the third dream?"

A woman's voice resonated from speakers overhead and to either side, "Fifteen of us have had the same experience?"

Jacob said softly, "My patient."

Elena recalled the woman's name, and replied, "Agatha, can you hear me?"

"Perfectly."

"It would be helpful if you would allow us to show your face."

"That cannot happen," the woman replied crisply.

"All right. But if any of you others feel you might be willing to reveal yourselves, it can only help." Elena waited, but all of the screens remained blue. She added, "We are all here for the same purpose. To confirm a warning that has come to us through these dreams."

To her astonishment, the one screen that switched from blue to a live feed revealed the face of United States Senator Mario Suarez. A murmur swept through the room. Suarez glared angrily at them from his position atop the rear wall and said, "This is going to destroy me."

"It is a risk we are all taking, sir," Jacob replied.

Mario glared not at the journalists but at the other blank screens. "Trevor, you can only hide out there for so long."

The only response was confusion from the faces on the other screens.

Senator Suarez snorted. "Coward."

"No one has called me that, not in forty-seven years."

"Well, then."

The face of SuenaMed's CEO flashed onto the screen. He scowled at Mario Suarez and said, "Senator, you just lost my support."

Elena turned back to the astonished journalists and the glaring television lights. "I think we can begin now."

Elena allowed the questions to continue for almost an hour, until all the major issues had been covered and the journalists began repeating themselves. She then rose and firmly concluded the conference. While people were still milling about afterward, Elena excused herself and slipped out the doors. Rachel caught up with her by the elevators. "Where are you going?"

"I have a class to teach this afternoon."

"But we're not done here!"

"I am."

Rachel waved back at the gathered journalists. "There are fourteen dreamers online who need your guidance."

"My response is the same as when we spoke on the phone. I can act as spokesperson for what has happened. But I cannot offer anything else unless I feel divinely guided."

Rachel flushed. "I wish you wouldn't insist upon bringing your God into this."

"Our God," Elena corrected. "From my perspective, there is no alternative."

"But these people *need* you."

"Again, I must respectfully disagree."

Jacob pushed through the conference doors, spotted them, and rushed over. "You're leaving?"

"I have to hurry back if I'm to make my afternoon class."

"Can I come with you? I have to get back to Atlanta. But I can fly from Melbourne as easy as from here."

Rachel was incensed. "*Both* of you are leaving?"

"I have professional responsibilities, just like you." Elena had an idea. "Can you set up a conference link and feed it to my computer?"

"I suppose . . ."

"If you want me to speak with the others, why not arrange an online conference call for tomorrow morning." Elena halted further argument by stepping into the elevator.

When the doors shut on Rachel's irritated expression, Jacob asked, "Would you rather I not come with you?"

"It's not that." She spoke carefully, feeling her way. "Melbourne

is more than my home. It is my refuge, my place apart from everything that's building out here. In the world. I need a space that is
separate. Where I can pray. And reflect. And seek guidance."

Jacob was silent as the doors opened and they crossed the elegant lobby. When they entered the humid Florida day, he said,
"Yesterday I asked Rachel why she was calling me and not you.
She said the idea of foretelling dreams linking strangers around
the globe was already staggering. Adding God to the mix would
make it impossible to pass on this warning."

Elena started down the sidewalk linking the building to the
visitor's parking lot. She saw no need to respond.

Jacob sighed. "This is very hard for me. I have spent my
entire life responding defensively to any mention of religion."

"We are talking about faith," Elena corrected. "At its best, religion is a matter of creating an earthly structure in which to express the wonder of connecting with the divine. At its worst,
religion seeks to fit God into a safe and comfortable little box.
Faith is man's individual walk with the Lord. This has everything
to do with faith, and almost nothing to do with religion."

Jacob glanced over. "My father would love talking with you."

She beeped her Jeep's doors. And waited.

"I could not get yesterday's conversation out of my head.
That and all the things I disliked most about your book and what
it implied." Jacob's gaze held a naked appeal. "I was hoping to
talk over these things with you."

"In that case, you would be most welcome to drive back with
me." Elena reached into her purse. "But first I need to make a call."

When Jacob rose from the Jeep an hour later, most of the female
students turned and stared. He had lived with his looks long
enough to ignore the attention, or so it seemed to Elena. He
glanced around and said, "The campus is lovely."

"This side contains the new money and buildings. The older portion of the campus is pretty basic."

He fell into step beside her. "My first gig after grad school was teaching at the Community College of Denver. The student population had doubled in less than three years. My classroom and office were in a pair of ancient mobile homes. The floors bucked and the lights flickered. A hard sneeze could blow out a window. I was there two years and thought I'd never get out."

"I wouldn't mind spending a few years here," Elena said. She wanted to add, *if I am allowed,* but held back.

He surveyed the lake, with its tall central waterspout and border of blooming oleander. "Who is this we're meeting with?"

"Reed Thompson is the university president. And a new friend." She led him down the central walk flanked by imperial palms and entered the main cafeteria. They crossed the atrium with its tall windows overlooking the lake, and entered the side alcove marked FACULTY ONLY. Reed was on his phone. He saw them enter and raised one finger.

"I've seen him somewhere," Jacob said.

"He was formerly the White House's chief economic adviser."

"Of course. Sure. I attended a conference where we both spoke." He looked at her. "I still don't understand why we are here."

"Reed is a trusted colleague, another professional, and a fellow believer."

Jacob's smile became slightly canted. "You mean, he's your backup."

"If you feel that way, we can leave and talk alone after my class. It's just, you and I share an awkward history. I thought including Reed might help."

"I don't know . . ." He looked beyond her. "Here he comes."

Reed introduced himself and ushered them back to the table by the window. He offered coffee, served them himself, then took the seat opposite Jacob and said, "How do we proceed?"

"I have real reservations about this," Jacob said.

"I understand fully."

"I mean, including you in this conversation. No offense intended."

"None taken. But I have to say, if I'd been in Elena's position, I would have done the same."

"You mean, with our history."

"That plays a part. But I was speaking of the here and now. You two are at the eye of a hurricane. Turbulent issues, a grave crisis, emotions running very high. Talking about God means adding another highly charged issue." He gave Jacob an opportunity to object, then asked, "When a couple comes to you in turmoil, what role do you play as a psychologist?"

Elena supplied, "The objective voice."

"But neither of you are objective," Jacob retorted. "Not about God."

"I am as objective as you are when you deal with the couple, given your training and your knowledge. You offer a different perspective, a different wisdom. So do I." Reed smiled. "I suggest there are further similarities. In counseling, you deal with both the present situation and related issues from the past. I will make just one more suggestion; then if you want to go, I completely understand. All right?"

"Yes. Go ahead."

"Dr. Rawlings, you contacted Elena and are seated here now, because you feel that your analytical stance is no longer satisfactory. Your current situation requires a clearer grasp of what is behind the veil of measurable reality." Reed's approach was utterly calm, he might as well have been discussing the weather.

"To understand God is to *know* him. You must experience the reality for yourself. Cross the line."

Jacob pondered that a long moment, before jerking a tense nod. "I'm listening."

Elena did not so much rise to her feet as allow herself to be lifted. "I need to go teach my class."

14

Elena emerged two hours later to find Jacob had already left for the airport and Reed had departed for an off-campus meeting. She did not care. She was exhausted from all the day had contained. She went home, ate a quick meal, and was asleep before sundown. She was woken twice during the night by rumbles, but when she realized it was thunder and not internal quakes from another dream, she swiftly returned to sleep.

The next morning Elena was reading her Bible on her balcony when the phone rang and Vicki said, "Is your television on?"

"It's six thirty in the morning."

"You think I don't know that? I haven't been up this early since before our son learned to sleep through the night." Her New York editor sounded impossibly chipper. "Sunrises are a ghastly affair, if you ask me."

"It's lovely down here."

"All those colors. Bad for the eyes. Is it on?"

"Yes."

"Turn to MSNBC. Hurry."

The financial reporter was saying, "It's not quite two in the morning in Lisbon. Rumors are swirling. The emergency cabinet meeting broke up an hour ago. Word on the street is, the national government has voted to withdraw from the euro and renege on its debts. In Japan, where the markets have already opened, the euro has fallen by fifteen percent. Stocks of banks exposed to Portuguese bonds have plummeted, pulling down off-hours trading to lows not seen since—"

Elena cut off the television and pressed a fist to her stomach. Her previous calm was replaced by a dread so great she felt nauseated.

Vicki said, "I had to go online to watch your press conference. The national news chose to ignore your clutch of dreamers, even with a US senator and the SuenaMed head honcho, what's his name?"

Elena swallowed. "Trevor Tenning."

"Those two looked like they'd had grilled cockroaches for breakfast." Vicki chuckled. "But word kept spreading. Our in-house techies have been going nuts. By midnight, the press conference was a viral phenomenon. An hour ago YouTube announced you had taken over the premier spot. Girl, you've had almost four million hits."

"It isn't me."

"It is as far as my people are concerned. This is beyond big. My board will let you write your own check if you'll do a book on this."

"Do you realize what you're saying? We have *no idea* where this is headed."

Vicki went quiet. When she resumed, her tone had grown somber. "Keep a journal. Make careful notes. Plan on turning this into a book. People will want to know. That is, assuming there is a tomorrow."

*   *   *

Two hours later, Rachel caught Elena just as she was leaving for class. "The press is demanding another conference."

"But there wasn't any dream last night. Was there?"

"Not that I'm aware. You've heard about Portugal?"

"Yes."

"They feel like everything has changed as a result."

"I don't see what we can offer. We've already answered every possible question. They can air what they have on tape."

"Trevor and the senator both agree with you." Rachel gave an exasperated sigh. "The dreamers have asked for us to set up the online conference as you suggested."

Behind the request she felt the pressure of future actions, one after the other, and yet she still had no sense of guidance or even of calm. "I need Jacob Rawlings to be involved."

"He is not the world authority on dreams. You are."

"His work made the initial connection among our colleagues." Her voice echoed as she descended the concrete stairway leading to the parking lot. "Not to mention his own patient is one of the senior officials experiencing these dreams."

"Who is that, by the way?"

"I can't divulge names, sorry."

Rachel sniffed. "All I know is, he publicly denounced your work before the professional world. He *insulted* you."

"Not anymore." Elena crossed the parking lot and beeped open her car door. "And having a second counselor participate can be very helpful in maintaining a steady course."

"Very well." Rachel's voice turned brisk. "Reginald has managed to speak with all the dreamers. The best time for the online conference call would be six thirty tomorrow morning."

Elena started her car and turned the AC on high. "I will make that work."

"Reginald will send you an e-mail with instructions. Now then. I've received several urgent requests for one-on-one interviews."

Elena slipped the car into gear. "No."

"You are seen as the group's official spokesperson. You are the recognized authority. People need a face they can put to this crisis. Someone who can help them understand—"

"I don't understand any of this," Elena replied. "Not the dreams or their purpose."

"Then you will tell them precisely that," Rachel replied.

"I already have."

"They need to hear from someone who can discuss this in a logical, professional manner. You are the only one out there." Rachel hesitated, then added, "Elena, please. They *need* you."

Just before eleven, Elena entered a packed lecture hall. Every seat in the banked auditorium was taken. More students lined the rear wall and the side rows. The buzzing conversation abruptly cut off at her entry. As she climbed the two low stairs to the wooden platform holding the dais and the whiteboard, the rear doors opened once more and Reed Thompson entered, followed by the provost and Elena's immediate superior, the head of the psychology department.

Elena set out her lecture notes, fighting the dreaded prospect of being fired once more. She stared at her hands as they rested on her carefully prepared sheets, and offered a silent prayer. She then bundled up her planned lecture and replaced the pages in her briefcase.

She put on as brave a face as she could muster and smiled at the class. "I can't imagine what you would like me to discuss today."

As soft laughter spread across the room, Elena used the

broadest pen and wrote on the whiteboard, *Dream Analysis*. She ignored the ripple of anticipation and went on, "Most of the leading figures in my field do not consider the analysis of dream content a valid science. Many psychologists tend to treat it with the same disdain as alchemy. I will discuss their objections another day. All I will say today is that Dr. Jacob Rawlings was until recently a leading opponent of dream analysis. He is in the process of changing his mind."

A young woman in the second row raised her hand. Elena said, "Yes?"

"Is he as good-looking in person as he is on television?"

"I saw him yesterday," another woman said. "He's a major hunk."

When the laughter died, Elena said, "We need to hold to a tone of professionalism. This is especially true with discussing dream analysis. Opponents will use any excuse to discredit the entire field. As I know from bitter experience."

She swiftly filled the whiteboard with the standard table her colleagues used in dream analysis. "I suggest you take notes, as this will be covered in your exams."

She knew she had adopted the coldly formal tone she had used in front of the cameras. It was a reflexive response to the three men standing by the rear doors. There was nothing she could do about it. As she wrote, she explained, "These are the two key models currently used in analyzing dream phenomena. This first row contains the most widely accepted breakdown of dream sequences: instigation, visual imagery, delusional belief, bizarreness, emotion, repressed memories, and uncovered meanings. The second row is the explanation offered through psychoanalysis, and the third row contains what is called activation-synthesis. This is a more recent approach, championed by professionals who seek to combine psychological and biological trends. So here we see under the heading, visual imagery, the psychoanalyst would interpret this as a regression to sensory levels, while the activation-synthesists would describe this as an activation of higher or subconscious visual centers."

Elena had long yearned to apply the rigor of her profession to a full scrutiny of dream analysis. For decades her colleagues had met in quiet corners at professional conferences and spoken of this only with a trusted few, knowing full well that if they went public, they would face the same derision and condemnation as she had known.

Forty minutes into the lecture, she asked for questions. A somber young man in the fourth row asked, "How do you explain these dreams on the news?"

She had known this was coming from the moment she wrote the first words on the board. Now that it was here, she found herself filled with a deep sense of calm resolve. "If you strip away all the sensationalism, what we are dealing with is known as foretelling. This concept is often met with derision among psychologists. The reason for this is simple. Virtually every long-term study of dreams has revealed that foretelling is far more common than previously recognized, particularly among people of strong faith. By this I mean people who pray regularly, are part of a community of believers, and study the Bible."

She ignored the resulting buzz of conversation, cleaned her carefully prepared summary from the board, and wrote the name *Sigmund Freud.* "The father of modern psychoanalysis was an opponent of any notion of God. He restricted his view of human nature, and dreams, to two essential components, which he called simply 'us and them.' The body and the external world. The ego and the id. The individual brain and the outer environment. Freud saw dreams as an unconscious attempt by the mind to work through events and emotions that were imposed on it by the external world. Nothing more. He was vehemently opposed to any concept of a divine force at work. His rejection of religion was so vicious that some contemporary analysts suggest it was actually a phobia. Freud wanted a dream state that was observable, subject to human analysis and control. To inject the divine into this meant there were things a scientist could neither predict nor analyze. So, as far as Freud was concerned, it simply did not exist."

Elena capped her pen, set it on the podium, and finished, "With respect, I disagree. Freud's severance of this link blinds us to a wealth of possibility and understanding. The evidence may be swept under the carpet. But the evidence is still there. The dream states contain remarkable insights into a linkage between the physical world and what lies beyond."

She lifted her hand to block a hundred further questions and said, "Class dismissed."

The three men moved against the tide heading for the exit. As they descended the stairs, one of the students who clustered around Elena asked, "What's going to happen next?"

"I have no idea."

"But one of the other dreamers, he's saying things are going to get worse."

"When was this?"

"I saw it on the news just before class."

"I can't answer for anyone but myself. The dreams are very vivid. They do not talk about steps beyond the one image. I personally think offering predictions beyond this one image is extremely dangerous."

Reed Thompson interrupted. "Elena, could we have a word?"

The president's formal tone caused the remaining students to fade away. Elena took a grip on the podium and waited. Her fears grew into a tense knot at the center of her gut.

The head of the psychology department was an older gentleman whose face beneath his graying beard had begun to descend like hot tallow. "I congratulate you on a most remarkable lecture, Dr. Burroughs."

She did not trust her voice, so made do with a nod.

"I don't know what I expected to hear, but your professionalism rang through." He hesitated, then added, "I must tell you, I was opposed to your hiring. I thought it was little more than a publicity stunt, something Reed hoped might lift our college's profile. I warned him that this might well blow up in our faces. When I first heard of this recent issue, I thought my worst fears had been realized."

He examined her as he would a bit of new evidence that had disproven his thesis. He said reluctantly, "I have been wrong before. I will no doubt be wrong again. Now if you will excuse me, I have a class of my own to teach."

Reed watched him leave with a thoughtful expression. "He ran my Sunday school class until his wife became ill. I've had the impression ever since I arrived here that he preferred to keep a tight separation between his faith and his profession."

"At least he has a faith," Elena replied.

"You threaten him," Reed said. "You push him outside his comfort zone."

"Then why did you bring him today?"

"I wanted him to see you at work."

"You had no idea what I was going to say. You couldn't. I didn't know myself."

"I didn't need to," Reed replied. "I know you."

Elena felt her face redden. Then she noticed how the provost was looking back and forth between the two of them, his head canted slightly. He smiled at some secret joke. Elena's face grew redder still.

Reed went on, "Tonight is my daughter's birthday. Will you join us?"

"She probably doesn't want to share you."

"Stacy asked me to invite you."

"Did she?" Elena saw the provost smile, and felt her face grow redder still. And she did not care. "I would be delighted."

They dined at D'Jon's, an upscale restaurant in the historic island village. The two dozen bayside houses dated from the nineteenth century. The restaurant had formerly been the residence of a pineapple plantation, back when Melbourne Beach was connected to the mainland by a little steam train. Five days a week the train pulled flatbed cars piled with fruit and avocados across the wooden bridge and then south to the Fort Lauderdale port. Weekends the produce cars were replaced by miniature passenger wagons. Working-class families strolled along the white sand or swam at the two beaches, one for men, the other for women and children. That evening Elena dined on fresh Atlantic grouper and joined in the conversation about everything under the sun, except dreams.

Stacy played the grown-up. This was her night, and she loved it. Her makeup was far too heavy for a girl her age. She wore a sheer black Valentino dress—a gift from her father and bought when he was not around, Reed assured Elena. In the candlelight and the soft laughter, Elena glimpsed the woman who should have been seated in her own chair.

The evening flowed beautifully, and was capped by father dancing with daughter to the music of a jazz pianist and an upright bass player. Elena watched and smiled and felt a subtle pang—not for the life she and her late husband had once known. Rather, for all these new future hopes.

As they left the restaurant, Reed turned on his phone and excused himself to check his messages. Elena resisted the urge to tell him to wait, to not permit the world entry. Stacy seemed to accept it as part of her father's life and responsibilities.

She and Stacy crossed the street and walked out the long city pier. A plaque stated this was a remnant of the old railway bridge, destroyed in 1917 by a hurricane. By the time World War I had ended and the town could rebuild, the world had moved on. A lone fisherman sat at the end, dipping his cane pole into the night-clad water.

Stacy leaned over the rail and said, "That guy with you on television looks cute."

"Jacob Rawlings is more than cute," Elena replied. "He's gorgeous."

"Do you like him?"

"Before all this started, I would have laughed at such a question. He publicly humiliated me. He represents the part of my profession I most dislike."

"And now?"

"I don't know."

"Daddy . . ." Stacy sighed.

Elena leaned on the railing next to her. They stared at the causeway bridge, rising from the black waters like a light-flecked ribbon. "Your father is a wonderful man. And you are one amazing young lady."

"Do you think, well, you and Daddy could ever . . ."

It was a night for secrets and intimacy, the warm breeze drifting across her heart with feather strokes. "I've had years of experience deflecting that question, even from myself. Ever since my husband died. Then last year I met a man in Rome, and my heart woke up again. It didn't work out with Antonio."

"What happened?"

"Life took us and spun us in two different directions."

"That's sad."

"It is and it isn't. Looking back, I feel as though his world and mine would never have fit as well as we might have liked. I truly dislike the spotlight. Ever since Antonio accepted his current role, he has seldom left it." Elena spoke across the dark waters, to the future she could only hope might someday come. "The nicest result of our time together is feeling like my heart has woken up. I would so very much like to love again."

As Elena walked back to where Reed Thompson still talked on his phone, the streetlight caught Stacy's face in a flash-forward of the woman she would soon become. Elena's breath caught in her throat at the awakening woman, and the wonder of being included in such a lovely moment.

Her phone's buzzing caught her by surprise. "I thought I cut that off." She checked the readout, and said, "I'm sorry, I need to take this."

"It's that guy, isn't it? The hunk."

Elena felt her face flame as she stepped away. "Jacob?"

Behind her, she heard Stacy repeat the man's name, "Jay-cob."

"Something's happened. I need you to come up to Atlanta."

"What's the matter?"

The man sounded impossibly tense. "I can't discuss it on the phone. I've gone ahead and booked you onto the first flight tomorrow."

She turned in a slow circle. Across the street from where she stood, flickering gas lamps lined the walk leading to the restaurant. The calm and pleasant meal might as well have taken place on the other side of the world. "Can't you at least say—"

"No, Elena. I can't tell you anything. You need to trust me on this. Will you come?"

15

At a quarter to six in the morning, the Melbourne airport was an island of calm. The wind was still, the air cool enough to be refreshing. Birds chirped from the tall palms forming a border between the parking area and the terminal. The loudest sounds were a taxi's radio and the rumbling of suitcase wheels across uneven pavement. Elena exchanged goodmornings with another woman headed for the entrance. Then she entered the terminal, and was assaulted by the sight of her own face. Television monitors fronting the café entrance blared the news channel, which played a repeat of the previous evening's story. The woman who had smiled at her outside glanced at Elena, then back at the monitors. She asked, "Should I cash out my 401K?"

"I have no idea," Elena replied.

"It's all my husband and I have."

"I don't know more than you do," Elena replied. "I can't extrapolate from the dreams."

The woman's gaze tightened on Elena. "This isn't about *extrapolation*. It's about our *future*."

"Sorry." Elena turned and walked to the counter.

She checked in, went through security, and found a quiet corner of the waiting area. With the end of the space shuttle program, Melbourne's airport had become quieter still. Only a handful of flights were arriving and departing. Most of the gates were silent. The empty departures lounge was lined by televisions tuned to the local news channel, which now showed an excited weatherman describing the tropical storm aimed at the Bahamas. The station's computer tracking models showed the storm gathering force and striking Florida's Atlantic coast as a category four hurricane.

Elena sat where she could look out over the runway and the sunrise. She opened her laptop, fitted on her headphones, and swiveled the microphone in front of her mouth. She was comfortable with the practice, since a growing number of professional conferences were scheduled online; though she wished she could participate in a more private environment. But Jacob's concern and tension had offered no alternative.

As the computer booted up, she pulled the handwritten notes from her purse and went through Reginald's instructions for linking into the company's secure conference call. The Suena-Med logo filled the screen. A chime sounded, followed by one image after another replacing the logo, like a series of dominos being laid out. Many of the spaces remained blank, filled instead by the same blue backgrounds and city names as during the news conference. Jacob's appearance in the top right corner filled her with a sudden sense of relief, though the man looked as if he had not slept a wink.

Reginald's voice asked, "Elena?"

"I'm here."

"Everyone who is able to join us today has linked in."

Elena asked, "Rachel?"

There was silence, then, "Yes."

"You need to turn on your camera and visually participate."

"I am not a dreamer."

"You are a primary facilitator," Elena replied, taking a term from her clinical work. "They need to know who you are."

The SuenaMed CEO said, "I agree with Dr. Burroughs."

There was a pause, then the bottom row tightened sufficiently to allow one more image to appear. Rachel's face showed deep displeasure.

Elena introduced Rachel, then asked, "Has anyone had another dream?"

There was a chorus of negative responses. Elena said, "Despite the fact that none of us has received any further image, I understand someone has been talking to the press. Making predictions about what will happen next."

Mario Suarez, senator from Miami, snapped, "That is beyond insane."

A heavyset man with a distinctly Australian drawl replied, "So what, we're supposed to just sit on our hands and wait?"

Trevor Tenning replied, "That is *exactly* what you are supposed to do."

An argument broke out online. Elena let the disagreement bounce from one electronic image to the next, and was about to insert herself, when she spotted movement out of the corner of her eye. The woman who had approached her at check-in walked to the window several rows away. She frowned at Elena and started toward her.

Elena felt helplessly exposed. She could almost see the woman's anger rise like heat waves off the runway. But she was held in place by the conference and the laptop and the headphones. She was about to drop everything and bolt, when a man she had not even noticed rose from the next row. He was a human fireplug, short and bulky and dressed in a nondescript blue blazer. He stepped over so that he blocked the woman's approach. The woman broke into an irate protest. The man gripped her arm and pulled her away. Only when they moved out of Elena's field of vision did she realize she had been holding her breath.

Mario Suarez chose that moment to bark, "All right, I've heard enough. I don't know about the rest of you, but I have responsibilities pressing in from a hundred different directions. We have reached as close to an agreement as we can. Anyone who makes any predictions that are not directly tied to further dreams is going to be stomped on by everyone else in the group. Agreed?"

The Australian protested, "I still say—"

"We know what you've said, and we're not covering that ground again. Are we in agreement?"

There was a chorus of assents. Then a pudgy man with a heavy French accent spoke from the bottom left corner. "What if all this is, you know, a joke?"

For those who refused to show their faces, a light framed their blue squares when they spoke. A vacant square in the middle of Elena's screen went bright, and a distinctly East Asian voice said, "*Joke?* My country's economy is *crumbling!*"

"No, I mean, I've tried every drug known to man. I've seen the mandalas. I've watched the walls move. What makes this any different? So we've all had the same dream. So what?"

The Asian man's rage crackled through her headphones. "I do not take *drugs.*"

"The bloke's got a point," the Australian drawled.

The Frenchman went on, "We're all watching the same lousy news. Who's to say we are not all victims of the same . . . what is the word I need?"

"Mass hysteria," Jacob replied, shaking his head. "It does not fit."

"Why is that, please?"

"Because the dreams are too precise. Plus, the images are not universal in nature. By this I mean there are certain symbols the human subconscious uses to interpret certain effects. In the dreams recorded thus far, none of these symbols is present."

"Not one?"

"Sorry."

The Asian voice demanded, "Then where do these dreams come from?"

When the silence had stretched on for a long moment, Jacob said, "Dr. Burroughs?"

"In dreams, we all enter mystery worlds," Elena replied. "It is a powerful and universal experience. One that defines the human psyche. The question as you have rightly stated is, where do these specific dreams originate? Either there is a higher power at work, or we are somehow . . ."

When she went silent, the Frenchman pressed, "Yes?"

An idea flitted around the recesses of her mind. She had started to say, either God was at work, or they were being manipulated. But how? Theoretically it was possible, but there was no concrete method to make it happen.

"Dr. Burroughs?"

She drew her racing mind back to the discussion. "Regardless of possible alternatives, we should do nothing unless we all experience another dream."

A blue square lit up and a woman's voice said, "I agree."

One of the blue squares cried, "But I want these nightmares to *stop!*"

The Asian snapped, "Forget your dreams. What about the economy?"

A blue square lit up and a woman's voice said, "What about my *country*?"

Suarez demanded, "Isn't there anything more you can offer us, Dr. Burroughs?"

"The only way I can speak of what lies beyond our experiences is if I receive divine guidance," Elena replied. "I continue to pray. But so far I have received no answer. Does anyone else on our panel believe in a living God?"

Her question was answered by a stony silence. Elena continued, "To do anything or say anything more would be just my own puny mind and ego at work. Just another human struggling with the unknown. That would be extremely dangerous for everyone."

The meeting broke up then. The final three images on Elena's screen were Rachel, Jacob, and Senator Suarez. Rachel snapped, "There was *no* need to bring God into this."

"With respect, I disagree."

"We need to maintain a professional atmosphere!"

"Again, with respect, I disagree," Elena said.

Rachel's fury seemed barely contained. "Reginald has made arrangements for you to be interviewed on CNN while you're in Atlanta."

"I'm not sure—"

"I wasn't asking your opinion. Reginald will be in touch."

When Rachel cut the connection, Jacob grimaced in sympathy and said, "Have a good flight."

The last person to sign off was the senator. To Elena's surprise, the man's anger was gone for once. Instead, he nodded and silently mouthed a single word.

Soon.

Jacob waved at her from beyond the security checkpoint at the Atlanta airport. The psychologist did not look at all well. His features were slack, his gaze as metallic as his voice. "How was your flight?"

"Fine. Jacob, what's the matter?"

"Not enough sleep, a life out of control." He did his best to effect a smile. "Same old, same old."

"Maybe you should get away for a couple of days."

"That's not happening, not with everything . . ." He waved it aside. "Any luggage?"

"Just my briefcase."

"Then let's go. I have a car waiting for us in the tow-away zone."

He led her through the airport at a trot. When they slipped into his Infiniti, he said, "Elena, meet Bryan. Bryan is one of my grad students."

"Yesterday I was a grad student," the young man corrected. "Today I'm a chauffeur."

Elena asked, "What's the rush, Jacob?"

His gaze flicked toward Bryan, then back. "Give it just a few more minutes. Bryan, anything?"

The student handed Jacob a cell phone. "A lady named Rachel called. Twice. Dr. Burroughs is confirmed for eleven at the CNN headquarters."

Jacob coughed, which turned into a rasping wheeze. "Elena, did you get that?"

"Yes. Jacob, what's the matter?"

"Things are heating up. Colleagues from around the world are calling to question my sanity. Last night as I left my house I was attacked by a dozen fringe types who accused me of plotting the end of the world. I would have been mauled if Rachel's body-guards hadn't pulled them off." He glanced around at her. "So you didn't dream anything last night?"

"No. Not for two days now."

"That's one bit of good news, I suppose."

Elena nodded, and wished she could agree.

They pulled into the parking lot of an upscale strip mall. A spa anchored one end, a cosmetic surgery facility the other. Pillars supported a curved glass roof over the main walkway. When they were parked, Elena said, "Bryan, could you give us a moment, please?"

"No problem." He opened his door. "Nice meeting you, Dr. Burroughs. I loved your book."

When they were alone, she said, "I don't like going into this cold, Jacob."

"They insisted on the secrecy. One of the people waiting for us is my patient, Agatha Hune."

"The Federal Reserve bank board member."

"Right. Agatha has someone she wants us to meet. Who, I have no idea. Only that he is a close personal friend. And it had to be this morning." He saw her objection forming, and responded before she could speak. "These people do not waste time, Elena. Agatha said it was utterly vital that we meet. I trust her. You're here. Let's go."

They entered the regional office of a US congressman whose name Elena did not recognize. A young staffer was there to open the door and usher them into a conference room. The unnamed guest turned out to be Mario Suarez. The senator was on the phone as they entered. He waved a greeting and pointed them into chairs. An aide working in the corner behind the conference table reached forward and handed Suarez a document. He said, "Hang on a second, Herb, I've got the figures here in front of me. No, no, that won't work. You need to cut another fifty mil or we can't move forward. Okay. Good." Suarez punched off the connection, tossed the phone to his aide, and said, "Go tell Agatha we're ready to roll."

The aide bolted from the room. Suarez swept the documents away from the table in front of him and said, "This meeting is not happening. Understood?"

"Yes," Elena replied.

He rose from his seat as a woman entered the room. Elena

saw in that action a different side to the senator. He might be rigid, impatient, and perpetually irritated, but he held others in respect and had no trouble showing it. "Have you met? Agatha Hune, Dr. Elena Burroughs. This other guy you know, right?" The woman was in her late fifties and attractive in a severe manner. She wore a sleek gray suit with a pewter and alabaster lapel pin. She seated herself across from the two psychologists. "Hello, Jacob."

Suarez asked, "You want the guy to stay, right?"

"Jacob is crucial to this, in my opinion." She turned to Elena. "I very much like your questions and your direction, Dr. Burroughs. Particularly this morning. You were right to include the issue of faith."

"Whatever you say." Mario Suarez dominated the room with his sense of presence. "Look. I'm not here to lay a charm offensive on you, Dr. Burroughs. And I don't expect you to leap over to our side."

"I thought we were all on the same side here, Senator."

"Maybe. Maybe not. Agatha?"

"You go ahead. I'll chime in if necessary."

"Right. Dr. Burroughs, what I want you to do is consider, just consider, that you are being manipulated."

"Not just you, Dr. Burroughs," Agatha Hune said. "Every last one of us."

16

Elena confessed, "I've been wondering the same thing."

"And?"

"Realistically, I don't see how it could be possible. The distance between dreamers, the timing, the dream's precise vividness, the dream patterns, the absence of archetypes, the fact that none of the dreamers knew one another before this started. All this indicates to me that these dreams are an actuality."

The senator impatiently shifted in his chair, but remained silent.

Jacob added, "To impact a patient's dreams requires manipulation of the person's deepest subconscious. This usually requires hypnosis in conjunction with drugs. Though it flies in the face of my entire professional career, I agree with Elena."

"We're not suggesting that the dreams aren't real," Agatha Hune replied.

"We've both had the dreams," Suarez agreed. "We're not here to discuss how *real* they are."

"We have read your book," Agatha Hune went on. "We have studied your comments. We have observed you during the interviews and today's online conference. Mario met with you both in Miami. I have known Jacob for some time now. And this has led us to trust you with what we feel may be a very real threat."

The leather of the senator's chair squeaked as he shifted forward. "What if someone is playing us like their public marionettes?"

Elena looked from one to the other. "You mean they've discovered a method for dream manipulation?"

"Right."

Jacob said, "And they're applying this process to fifteen dreamers spread around the globe."

"Exactly."

Elena wanted to dismiss the idea. She disliked the senator's attitude and his manner. But the idea held her at a visceral level. "I don't see how that would be possible."

"Right. Neither do we." Mario Suarez nodded to his friend. "Tell them, Agatha."

"We have been hearing rumors. A hint of something here, a shadow of a whisper somewhere else. Then yesterday Mario's most trusted aide overheard comments. These things simply do not add up unless we accept one impossible fact: that someone is doing this for a secret purpose."

Elena asked, "What precisely did your aide overhear?"

"My aide was representing me at a conference of bank directors on Wall Street. They were discussing the crisis. I'm on the senate finance committee, it's normal for either me or my top committee aide to be there. At break time my guy was hidden in this alcove, texting me an update. Two of these Wall Street jokers passed by, he didn't see which ones they were and couldn't recognize their voices. What he heard was, one of the guys asked the other how the project was going. The other said, and I quote, 'You mean the market exploitation, or the dreamers?' The first guy said, 'Both.' Guy two then said, 'All but one of the dreamers are behaving themselves. As for the market, I should hope you're making a killing like the rest of us.'"

Elena looked from one face to the other, and saw grim intent. And very real fear. "So if this is true, the aim behind manipulating our dream states is to subvert the world economic system."

Jacob protested, "That suggests an incredible level of power behind their actions."

Agatha added, "And coordination among different groups. No lone bank or even political system could do this alone."

Suarez rose from his chair, and began crossing the back of the room, pacing like a caged beast. "When I was a kid, my grandfather used to tell us stories. My mother always objected because they gave me and my sisters nightmares. But my father insisted. He remembered the crossing from Cuba. And losing his own mother on the boat. And he wanted us to learn. After a while my sisters would run and hide whenever my grandfather started on his stories about life under Castro and what they went through in escaping to America. But I stayed. And I listened. I learned about how power drove some men mad. How they used the most insane reasons to excuse their actions. How the lives of others mean nothing to such people. How they build their ideals into golden calves, how they will sacrifice the lives of millions at the feet of their idols."

Suarez turned and glared at them. "I have learned from bitter experience that the world scoffs at politicians who trumpet their faith in God. So I don't speak about it except with my closest friends. But I know the Bible. I know the evil that lurks in this world. And I am telling you that in my heart of hearts, I think we have become trapped inside someone else's nightmare."

Elena met the man's burning gaze and found herself saying, "I have prayed and prayed for guidance. And all I have received in response is silence."

"As though God is not a part of this," Suarez agreed.

"What should we do?"

"We need your help," Agatha said. "Desperately."

"We've shared this with three of our most trusted aides, and nobody else," Suarez said. "Not even our families. We ask that you do the same."

"We're almost certain we're being watched," Agatha Hune confirmed. "If our fears are correct, you must assume they are keeping you both under surveillance."

"They need us, so they fear us," Suarez said.

"If we're right," Agatha corrected. "If we are indeed part of a hoax."

The word hung there in the air between them. Elena found herself surprised at her own calm. As though she was glad for the company of those who also felt a need to question. "So we shouldn't contact you?"

"Only when there is a critical need, or you have something to report," Suarez replied. "And you'll need a cutout."

Agatha said, "She doesn't understand that word."

"I do, actually. You want me to find someone they won't suspect, who can make the contact for me." Elena thought. "I have just the person."

"Our aides will be hunting for more evidence," Agatha Hune replied, sliding a card across the table. "If you find anything that suggests we are right, you can reach us day or night."

"You're both professionals," Suarez said. "Clinicians, isn't that what you want the world to see? So design an experiment. Check your data. See if there is a shred of evidence we're right."

"Before it's too late," Agatha said.

Suarez headed for the door, then turned back to give Elena a look of deadly experience. "If we're right, and I fear we are, remember this. There are people out there who will do anything and say anything and sacrifice anyone to get what they want."

17

Jacob gave his postgraduate student some bills and told him to grab a taxi back to the university. He and Elena made the trip downtown in silence. It was only as they left the freeway that Jacob asked, "What just went on back there?"

"I'm going to need some time to fully digest it."

"But you think it might be real?"

"*They* certainly think so. Two intelligent professionals on the world stage, one in politics, the other in finance, both suggesting this is *very* real."

"But to manipulate dreams around the globe—"

"Is impossible. I agree. Not to mention manipulating the world economy."

"So how—" Jacob was halted by the ringing of his cell phone. He glanced at the readout, then handed it over. "Answer that, will you?"

When she answered, Reginald Pierce said, "We've just heard from CNN. Don't go through their front doors. Come in by way of the garage. It's marked Employees Only, but just tell the security guard your names and they'll let you through."

The young man sounded impossibly tense. Elena demanded, "What's the matter?"

"The dreamer who claimed all this was garbage, you know who I mean?"

She recalled the pudgy Frenchman who had spoken with such disdain. "Actually, he just suggested our experiences were not foretelling."

"Well, he's using the word now. *Garbage.* On television. And his claims have gone global."

Nothing could have prepared her for what awaited them downtown.

The street fronting CNN headquarters was blocked off. Police had stationed yellow barriers across the turning. Beyond them was a solid wall of humanity. Jacob fought through the snarled traffic, rounded the corner, and finally arrived at the entrance to the underground parking garage. When he gave his name to the uniformed officer, the guard leaned over to give Elena a long look, shook his head, and waved them through. Elena turned in her seat to see him lift the phone and speak with someone, his gaze still on them.

The garage elevator deposited them in the main lobby. To her horror, Elena was surrounded by images of herself. She stared down from a dozen massive flat-screen monitors that lined the foyer and flanked both buildings overlooking the street.

"Dr. Burroughs?" A harried young man in a rumpled shirt pushed his glasses up square to his forehead. "Hi, I'm Jeff, they're ready for you—"

The crowd spotted her through the foyer's tall glass windows. A woman shrieked her name. The crowd picked it up and began hammering the glass. The young man said something she could not hear, and pulled them into an elevator. When the doors closed, he said, "The loonies have us under siege."

Jacob asked shakily, "How did they find out?"

"We posted your name on the online interview schedule. Our website is updated every few hours. It's normal."

"Nothing about that crowd out there is normal."

"No, what I mean is, her name was just there on the list. You know, 'Stay tuned to see Dr. Elena Burroughs live at eleven.' Like that. But this thing, it's just exploded in our faces." The doors opened. He directed them down the side corridor. People emerged and watched them from every doorway. "Makeup is down on your right, Dr. Burroughs."

"Isn't Dr. Rawlings appearing with me?"

"I've got it down as just you, Dr. Burroughs. But I could go ask."

"Yes. Do that. Please. And I need a word in private with Dr. Rawlings."

"Sure thing." He opened the makeup door and spoke quickly, and a young woman exited the room. "Just let her know when you're ready."

The makeup room was narrow and long, with a light-rimmed mirror taking up one entire wall. The waist-high counter was filled with every imaginable cosmetic and brush and hairspray. A stack of broad napkins anchored both ends. Elena slipped onto one white leather stool because her knees felt weak. "They have me going on *live*?"

"It sounded that way."

"On national television? Jacob, I don't have anything to say!"

"Be a professional. Tell them the truth. No varnish. Don't let them bully you into saying anything more than what you're comfortable—"

"Will you pray with me?"

He stared at himself in the mirror. But Elena was uncertain

what exactly it was he saw. His past, his reputation, his way of life. Whatever it was, she actually saw the change come over him. The intent manner in which he studied his own reflection, and the tightening of his features. "I'm not ready to take that step."

"I understand," she said softly.

"Maybe somewhere down the line. But I can't let all of this pressure me into doing something that doesn't feel right."

"Jacob, you don't have to explain. Would you tell them I need another moment, please?"

He realized he was being dismissed. He looked at her through the mirror, and started to say something more. She could sense the conflict behind his eyes. In the end, though, he simply nodded and left the room.

After he had left, Elena remained as she was for an instant, staring at the place where he had been. In her heart, she sensed a door softly closing.

She opened her phone and dialed the number from memory. When Reed Thompson came on the phone, Elena said, "I'm about to go live on CNN. I can't do this on my own."

"What can I do?"

"Pray with me."

His reply was immediate. "Let's bow our heads."

As soon as Elena's makeup was done, she entered the center of a maelstrom.

Because the news was fed live to the cable channel, the entire production unit hummed with a frantic energy. Yet the atmosphere was also extremely professional. There was no shouting, hand waving, or hysterics. What she saw were the glittering faces of people forced to run through every day chopping and slicing their waking moments into tight five-second bursts. And they loved it. The vast production space was filled with young people who were thrilled with their work. Even when they were extremely worried. Like now.

She was handed from one person to the next. All of them showed her a bright cheerfulness and hurried her along. She heard herself referred to as "the eleven-fifteen." As in, the time-slot she was slated to fill. They all knew her name; they knew the topic she was to discuss. They all said how glad they were she would make time for them. Elena had the impression they spoke the same words to a hundred different faces every day, and remembered none of them.

"Okay, Dr. Burroughs. I'm going to walk you out and sit you next to Betty. You should address your answers to her. Try not to look at the cameras at all." The woman was in her thirties, but under the glare of the television lights she had the tight-edged features of someone who had lived hard, pushed harder, and missed her big chance. She still wore her hair with the shellacked perfection of a person born for the camera's eye. But she had a clipboard and headphones and her ID said PRODUCTION. "You will be on for twelve minutes. It's best to keep your answers short and to the point. Any questions?"

Elena shook her head. She found herself isolated from the energy and the scene, and preferred not to speak.

But the woman took her silence for fear and said, "Everything is going to be good. We're on your side here, Dr. Burroughs. We just want to get the word out to as large an audience as possible. Okay?"

"Yes," Elena said, but mostly so the woman would not pester her anymore. Elena was held by a very strong sensation, as though she were shielded from not just these people and their agendas but the energy and the place as well. She moved among them, and yet they did not reach her. Not where it mattered.

If she had to put a name to it, she would have called it peace.

"Okay, here we go."

Elena was led onto a carpeted dais and up two steps to a curved desk of blond wood. The presenter of the nation's most watched television business news journal had half risen from her chair in order to see off her last guest. Then she turned and offered Elena the smile that had galvanized a thousand on-air arguments. "Dr. Burroughs, I have so been looking forward to meeting you."

"Commercials over in ninety," the producer said, moving away.

"It seems as though the whole world is talking about you and your little group. I thought we might begin with a late-breaking item from one of your dreamers, then allow you to respond. Is that acceptable?"

"Of course." The wall behind her chair was seamless glass shaded a pale aqua. Behind this were rows of computer terminals and staffers and researchers. All of them wore headphones. The far wall was lined by an LED ticker that streamed a constant flow of stock data. The atmosphere was in direct contrast to the newscaster's voice. This was part of her persona, the calm at the center of whatever storm happened to be brewing that day.

And today, it was Elena and the dreamers.

But Elena remained utterly removed from the pressure. Calm. Alert. And ready.

The woman must have noticed this. A steely glint entered her gaze. Clearly she enjoyed stripping away her guest's power or calm or whatever shield they had brought with them to reveal their hidden flaws and weaknesses to the public eye.

"Five seconds."

"Let's begin, shall we?" The woman turned to the camera, introduced herself, and then said, "Our next guest has suddenly appeared on the world stage, claiming to represent a cluster of dreamers who can foretell the future. Welcome, Dr. Elena Burroughs."

"Thank you."

"Tell me, Elena. Should I sell my shares of GM?"

"I can only describe what you have already heard. The dreams are very specific. To discuss anything further would be both wrong and potentially dangerous."

"And yet some of your little group are doing just that. Speaking out."

"They are not on this program. I am."

"Actually, one of them is." She turned to the camera and said, "Joining us from France is another dreamer who has quite a different perspective on what is going on here."

The pudgy face appeared on the feed to Elena's right. The young man showed a bitterly cynical attitude as he dismissed the dreams as a sham. Just another type of mass hysteria. He finished by declaring, "They tried to shut me up. But I'm not going along with their little charade a moment longer."

The newscaster turned back to Elena with a satisfied smirk. "Would you care to respond?"

"They are certainly free to form their own opinions. But these dreams do not follow any known pattern of hysteria."

"Would you explain?"

Elena found herself adopting the precision of a clinician facing a hostile audience. But gone was her former cold shield. It was no longer necessary. Instead, she was calm. Open. "I freely accept that we are in completely open territory. You and your viewers know the contents of what we have dreamed. I can't tell you anything else. We have shared these images out of concern for the world's economy."

"Wouldn't you say that such huge unknowns make these dreams highly dangerous? I mean, really, Dr. Burroughs. Think of the risk you are suggesting the world's leaders take, all because—"

"I'm not suggesting they do anything," Elena replied.

"But you just said—"

"The dreams are what they are. Given the pattern revealed by the Portuguese default, there is evidence to suggest they might hold some value. But that is all I can say."

"Your attitude is certainly very cavalier. 'Here's the answer to the world's problems. Do what you want.'"

"On the contrary; all we can say is what we have experienced."

"So you're telling us we must simply wait for the next deluge of bad news from *beyond*."

"This is not a game," Elena replied. "We can't say whether there will ever be anything more. We are simply reporting on what we have witnessed. Nothing more."

The newscaster disliked her inability to pierce Elena's shield, and it showed in how her smile turned brittle and her words took on a new bite. "It would seem to me that you and these other so-called forecasters are on a mad power trip."

Elena remained utterly untouched. It was, she knew, a living miracle. "You are wrong about this," she replied. "As you are wrong about everything else."

After the interview, Elena bade Jacob farewell and returned to the Atlanta airport by taxi. Jacob clearly wanted to take her, but Elena insisted. She felt utterly drained. She did not want to talk or even have any need to think. She closed her eyes to the city's snarled rush-hour traffic and drifted.

As she waited for her flight to board, Elena cradled her phone in her hands, debating whether to call Reed. She kept telling herself that she should at least thank him. But she was conflicted. And she was uncertain as to when his patience with her needs might run out. Then as she was boarding, the phone buzzed and Reed's number showed on the readout. She felt a sudden welling at heart-level and had to swallow hard before managing a hello.

"Are you all right?"

"Sort of. I guess. It's over, that's the most important thing."

"Where are you?"

"Waiting in line to board the flight home."

"Can I meet you?"

She started to protest. Elena had made a profession of standing on her own, of making do without the help of others. But her need to see him was so strong it broke through all the years of barriers, as if they had never even existed. "I can't think of anything I would like more."

The commuter jet was jammed. The plane held some thirty people in narrow seats. She spotted her two guards among those boarding and nodded a greeting. The pair seemed uncertain whether they should even acknowledge her. But she thought it was time to set aside all such casual artifices. Especially from herself.

She emerged from airport security to find Reed waiting as promised. She rushed over, wanting desperately to tell him about her day and so much else.

And suddenly found herself in his arms.

Elena gave herself fully to the embrace. She breathed in the smell of him. She found herself ravenous for the strength in his arms. She kissed him, a brief touch of lips upon lips, and thought she had never tasted anything so fine.

He looked at her then, and murmured, "Welcome home, Elena."

18

Elena had not eaten any dinner. The day's tension had left her without an appetite. But when Reed suggested they stop by his home for a bite, she suddenly found herself famished. Father and daughter refused her offer of help, and ordered her to relax. Elena walked through the home's front rooms. Large windows faced the circular drive, which was rimmed by lamps in handblown glass. The light through the gauze drapes was a soft gold in color. Elena entered the formal parlor and studied the oil painting on the side wall. She knew it had to be of Reed's late wife. In the dim light the image glowed and the eyes moved with her. Elena could well understand the questions behind the portrait's smile. She was asking the same questions herself.

Stacy's light footsteps sounded from the central hall. "Should I turn on some lights?"

"It's nice like this." Elena continued to study the portrait. "You are amazingly like your mother."

"She's so much more beautiful than me."

"I don't find that at all."

Stacy gave no indication she had even heard. "When I was little, I used to curl up on a divan they had in their bedroom back in Washington. It was between the bed and Mom's dressing table. I would sit there with this green turtle I used to carry everywhere. His name was Malcolm. And I'd watch Mom get ready. Dad was often somewhere doing something important. And Mom often joined him for the evening events. She taught European history at the American University. When I was born, she cut back to one class each semester, so she could spend time with me."

Elena slipped into a high-backed chair by the fireplace. Stacy went on, "Mom kept the baby quilt from my crib on the divan. It was the softest thing I had ever felt. I held that in one hand and Malcolm in the other and watched her get ready. She'd put on her makeup and dress and then bring the jewelry box over so I could help her choose what piece to wear. My favorite was a string of pearls she inherited from her grandmother when she was my age. She told me that every time she put them on. And someday she wanted to give them to my daughter."

Elena had to clear her throat before she could say, "Are those the pearls she is wearing in the painting?"

"Yes. I have them upstairs. In her jewelry box. I haven't ever worn them. Maybe someday." Stacy turned from the painting to look at Elena. In the half light her gaze was dark, ancient. "I haven't ever talked about that before. Not to anyone."

"I am so honored," Elena whispered.

"The year after Mom died, I woke up screaming one morning. I'd dreamed I couldn't remember who Mom was, or what she looked like. So Daddy . . ."

Elena swallowed hard. "Your father had this portrait done. And hung where you could always come and see her. Not where you had to look at her every day. But where you knew she was when you wanted to come and visit."

When Stacy turned back to the painting, the wet streaks on her cheeks reflected the light through the windows. "The artist asked me what I wanted most to see in the portrait. I told her, paint this portrait with the same care Mom used putting on her makeup before she went to meet Daddy. And show the love she always had for us."

Elena cleared her own eyes and waited where she was, giving the young lady the time and space to knit her world back together. She knew she would soon share a number of her own stories with Stacy. But not now.

Finally Stacy smiled and said, "Dinner's ready."

Elena had thought the moment could not be any more complete. Then as they reentered the kitchen, the young lady reached over and took Elena's hand.

They ate at the small breakfast table, set in a windowed alcove off the back of the kitchen. The table had only two chairs, so Reed brought a third in from the dining room. Elena ate with real appetite, and loved the sense of belonging. Over coffee she shared with them her experiences from the past few days. Twice she wondered if she took things too far, covering in depth such issues before Stacy. But Reed gave no indication that he objected, and Stacy certainly appeared to follow it all. And something more. Elena found herself observing the scene from a distance. As though she was both the person talking and an observer standing on the kitchen's other side. She saw she was not merely accepted, but welcomed.

As they cleared the table, Elena described how Jacob had refused to pray with her. How she had felt a door closing, one that had no handle on her side.

It was Stacy who finished the thought. "As though Dr. Rawlings is the only one who can open the door he closed."

"That is how it appeared to me," Elena agreed.

"I wonder how often God feels the very same thing," she said.

They stood there in the kitchen and prayed a final time, then Reed asked, "Will you be safe in your home?"

"SuenaMed has supplied me with a security escort."

Reed shook his head. "I can't get over how their CEO is one of the dreamers."

Elena kept her gaze on Reed, but the words were meant for his daughter. "A great deal of what I've shared with you is confidential."

"Stacy is a pro when it comes to keeping secrets," Reed assured her. "And so am I."

The wave of comforting calm accompanied Elena on her drive home. She smiled her way into bed, for once not even caring how tired she was. The sense of being surrounded by the strength and love of friends was that great.

Which only made the dream's arrival that night all the more savage.

The next morning Rachel called Elena to confirm that others had also suffered through another dream. Rachel then offered to send a SuenaMed limo for her. But Elena preferred to remain in control of where she went and how. And this morning Elena wanted the time alone, not just to separate herself from the dream, but more important to ponder how they might begin the hunt.

Her phone rang as she drove through the condo's gates. Elena pulled to the side of the road. As hoped, the call was from Reed. She connected and said, "Thank you for phoning me back. I'm sorry to have called so early."

"I'm the one who needs to apologize. I've been up for hours.

But I make a habit of not looking at my phone until after my quiet time."

"There's been another dream."

"You had it also?" Reed asked.

"We all have."

"Can you talk about it?"

By the time Elena was done, her voice had lowered to a clipped murmur. The telling was that hard.

Reed was silent for a long moment before asking, "Where are you?"

"Headed to Orlando. All the dreamers are gathering for an online conference call before we go public."

He pondered, then came back with, "I have a meeting this morning with the auditors that can't be put off. Would you like me to drive over and join you once that's done?"

"What about your other appointments?"

"Everything else can wait. Plus, I'd very much like to be able to help."

She released the fear and tension she had been carrying since the dream's onslaught. "In that case, there is nothing I would like more."

The company's front drive was rimmed by news vans. Security guards flanked an orange barrier holding back an army of cameras and newscasters and journalists. Reginald stood outside the SuenaMed entrance, nervously pacing beyond the phalanx of reporters. As soon as Elena rose from the car, the camera lights flashed on.

Elena was greeted by a hundred shouted questions. Reginald said something that was lost to the clamor. Elena followed him into the ornate lobby and was confronted by a dozen screens all showing her face. Everyone in the crowded foyer stopped and stared as she passed. Reginald gave no sign he noticed them. "Someone informed the press about the new dream. Ever since the news broke, CNN has played your interview on a continuous loop."

Which explained the half dozen calls Elena had received from Vicki Ferrell, her editor. Elena started to ask who was behind the leak, and decided it did not matter.

The elevator doors closed on the faces and the noise. Elena wished it were easier to breathe. Reginald asked, "Was the dream as bad as they say?"

"They're all bad. This one was . . . different." She studied his reflection in the bronze doors and asked softly, "What's wrong, Reginald?"

"Rachel took a call in her office. Now she's vanished. I can't find her anywhere."

That did not explain the trembling of his hands, or the nervous tic beneath one eye. "Reginald, look at me. What is really the matter?"

"All I have are rumors." He refused to meet her eye as the elevator doors opened. "The conference room is just across the hall."

Their conference call was one step off of a full-blown panic. Arrayed on a massive flat screen that dominated one wall of the conference room, the dreamers revealed their base natures, angry or panicked or teary or bossy in turn. Only two individuals remained removed from the noisy fray. One was Elena. The other was the CEO of SuenaMed. Trevor Tenning sat and frowned his way through the others' alarm. He gave nothing away.

Elena did not speak once. Instead, she spent much of the time reliving the dream itself, allowing the images to wash over her, feeling the dread and the intense pressure to speak and act anew. Only now there was something overlaid upon it all, a sense of being shielded from the worst of the fray. The longer she sat there, the more she became certain that Reed Thompson and his daughter were praying for her.

Elena stared at the dreamers on the flat screen and nodded at a few points she only half heard. Jacob served as moderator. Elena watched his subtle direction and knew there was nothing she could add to the man's highly professional management. She let the images sweep her away.

The dream had started the same as all the others. A shadowy messenger had appeared at her door. Elena wondered why she felt it necessary to answer his call and allow him to enter. But at a deeper level she knew she had no choice in the matter. It was like studying an image through rushing water. The dream had progressed to the same image as before. Elena had stood in a soup line. Only this time, the entire city was there with her. Everyone. The billboards that dominated the cavernous walls held the same two words, DISASTER STRIKES.

As she read the headline, all color washed from the dream. The result was a sepia image from the Great Depression, only this was now her reality. As the line gradually moved toward the counter, Elena knew there would not be any food left for her.

Suddenly the air was filled with the ringing of a church bell. Two booming tolls, counting down the days remaining before disaster. Elena knew this with utter certainty. The world had only two more days to act.

The other dreamers had received precisely the same impression. Two days.

Elena rubbed her face hard, trying to draw herself away from the dream and back to the ongoing discussion. The oval conference table reflected the fourteen images displayed on the massive flat screen. Only four figures remained blue now, the others having accepted that their voices needed a face. One of those who remained hidden was the Federal Reserve bank executive. As usual, Agatha Hune did not say a word. Rachel had not appeared. And Reginald Pierce had vanished after ushering Elena inside.

Jacob was seated to her right. He used a moment of loud wrangling to ask where Rachel was. Elena replied, "I have no idea."

"Is something the matter? I mean, between us."

Elena looked at him. Really looked. It all came back to that one missing element. The choice he had made.

But before she could reply, the conference room door opened and a very pale Rachel Lamprey announced, "I have some bad news."

When the faces on the screens stopped their bickering, she went on, "The French dreamer, Jacques Aines, is dead."

"We just received word," Rachel said. She was seated in the conference chair closest to the doorway. The people on the screen were silent, the faces watchful and frightened. "He suffered convulsions about six hours ago. He lives in the apartment next to his sister; she was there and saw it happen. The doctors think it was an epileptic fit, but he has no such history."

She went silent, her dark eyes staring blindly out the wall of floor-to-ceiling windows. Beyond the glass, another summer storm crept toward downtown Orlando.

When she appeared unable to continue, Reginald Pierce said softly, "He arrived at the hospital in a comatose state. He died soon after."

Rachel shook her head. "I can't believe this has happened."

Reginald looked at his boss. "This is not your doing. You're six thousand miles away."

The woman looked shaken to her core. "I feel responsible. For all of this."

"You've done all you possibly can for the dreamers," Reginald said. When she did not respond, he said more sharply, "You need to focus, Rachel."

She blinked and glanced at her watch. "The news conference should have begun half an hour ago."

"That's right," Reginald said. He looked at Elena in desperate appeal. "Will you handle this without her?"

She had been debating whether this was the moment to tell them that she was going to back out entirely. Instead, she heard herself say, "Of course."

But as they were signing off, Agatha Hune spoke for the first time. "Something has just come in. I'll read you what it says. The New England Bank of Hartford, the sixth largest financial institution in the US, has declared that it is temporarily unable to meet its obligations and is closing its doors. Federal inspectors are on hand to take over and assure an orderly dispersal of funds."

There was a moment's stunned silence, then a voice asked, "What does it mean?"

"It means our economy is tanking," another replied.

"No, no. What does it *mean*? If this isn't the thing that's coming in two days, what is?"

"Ruin," another participant muttered. "Disaster."

"We have to *do* something."

"That is absolutely correct." Reginald stepped to the teleconference controls. "The news conference is our next step. Elena?"

As she rose from her chair, Elena fastened her gaze on Mario Suarez. The senator's stare burned a hole through her heart.

19

Reed Thompson was waiting in her SuenaMed office when she emerged from the press conference. Elena shut the door and pressed the button by the light switch. The glass walls overlooking the interior work areas went opaque.

Reed shook his head. "Back in my power days, only a select few places had these. The Senate Intelligence Committee, the White House secure offices, and so forth. I heard they were everywhere these days. But it's still amazing to see."

Elena didn't want to discuss the high-tech walls. She wanted to hold him and be held. "I'm so glad you came."

When he finally released her, Elena took his hand and they walked to the elevators. When they emerged in the lobby, Jacob Rawlings stood there, clearly waiting for her. His surprise at seeing Elena and Reed together was evident. Elena felt Reed's fingers start to slip away, but she tightened her grip. She knew she would always remember this moment, holding Reed's hand and feeling the emotional connection, while Jacob observed them, his gaze tight. Elena suspected few women had chosen another man over Jacob Rawlings.

Jacob said, "I see."

The three of them left the building and walked into the oppressive afternoon. Jacob came because Elena insisted. She knew Reed would have preferred to release her hand, but she insisted on that too. It was time for action. She needed these men to be with her. Together. On her terms.

Elena said, "I have an idea and I need your help. Both of you."

The heat was almost stifling. The surrounding buildings blocked the afternoon breeze. Their steel-and-glass surfaces formed walls of shimmering mirrors. Reed Thompson squinted at the sunlit headquarters while Elena talked. Jacob stared at the grass and the flowers still damp from the passing storm. When she finished, Reed said, "This is a good plan."

"Jacob?"

"I can do this."

"I know you can. Will you?"

"Yes. All right." He hesitated, then asked, "What if Suarez is wrong and the dreams are for real?"

"We'll know in two days."

"Can we wait that long?" Jacob lifted his gaze to meet hers. "Can the world?"

She was about to try to explain what was happening at the core of her being. How the time of prayer and the company of believers seemed to be pulling her away from the dreams. How the previous day's conversation with Agatha Hune and Senator Suarez had helped crystallize these feelings. How she had already begun to withdraw from the group and its direction.

But Elena stopped before the words were formed, because Reginald Pierce emerged from the lobby's front entrance, spotted them, and hurried over. "Trevor Tenning wants to see you."

"Me? Now? Why—"

"He didn't tell me." The sunlight only heightened the man's

taut features. "Elena, he says to tell you that it is extremely important, and insists that you meet with him alone."

A litany of devastating financial news tracked Elena as she traversed the lobby. Reginald accompanied her to the penthouse, where they entered a frozen tableau. The normal clusters of intense discussions had been wrecked, the people drawn to the screens, which displayed a soft dirge of worry and fear. All of the heads turned to watch her progress, which was hardly a surprise, as Elena saw her own face there on the screens, flashed into acute clarity by the photographers.

Trevor Tenning's office was a study in contrasts. SuenaMed's CEO actually greeted her with a smile. "Reginald found you. Excellent. Thank you for coming. Please, won't you take a seat. Coffee?"

"No thank you."

He asked Reginald, "Were you able to locate Rachel?"

"She's still tied up with the conference call you were supposed to take. The one with Europe's licensing committee."

Trevor pursed his lips. "Perhaps we should delay our launch."

Reginald blanched. "The products are in place. Doctors have already begun writing prescriptions. Clinics all over the world—"

"All right." Tenning did not need to raise his voice to silence the young man. "But we could make it low-key. Hold off on all publicity until this has passed."

Elena realized, "You think the crisis will be averted."

Tenning used a finger to direct Reginald out of his office. When the door closed, he replied, "I don't think. I know."

"How is that possible?"

Tenning's smile was genuine. "Because I've had another dream."

Trevor Tenning related how his latest dream had come near dawn. After being assaulted by the first dream of the night, he had thought he was not going to fall back to sleep. He had actually gone downstairs to make a pot of coffee, then lay down on the sofa in his study and was gone. That was how he put it. He had shut his eyes and was transported into yet another dream.

Only this time there was no worry or despair or fear. Just the opposite. The dream had been so fine he had actually regretted its passage.

Elena sat across the desk and watched as the SuenaMed CEO's face effused an ethereal glow. She felt a deep disharmony, a conflict of sensations. On the one hand, she doubted what she was seeing. She could not help it. Up to this point, the dreams had all followed a distinct pattern. They came to everyone on the same night. And they had all been terrible to behold.

And yet, at the same time, Elena found herself vaguely jealous. Why should he be granted this and not her, or the rest of them? Because the light in his eyes, or the relaxed stance, or the smile, all of this seemed genuine.

Tenning's second dream had shown a way out. The world's banks needed to unite. Create one cohesive force, large enough to reintroduce a balance into the world's markets.

"It seemed so self-evident, once it was revealed," Tenning told her. "Only if the major financial institutions are to join together can we create a structure large enough to overcome this turmoil."

Elena asked, "Was that the end of the dream?"

Not quite. The combined banks issued their own currency. In his dream, Trevor Tenning had actually held one of the bills. Across its face were written the same words in an array of languages—*One World Currency*. As soon as his fingers had touched the money, Trevor had lit up with joy. He had woken with the same sense of bliss that creased his features now as he spoke. He had opened his eyes knowing that everything was going to be all right.

Elena pointed out, "But you frowned your way through the conference call. I've never seen you look so worried."

Tenning nodded approval at her comment. "Of course I was concerned that it was all a lie. I had experienced the night's first dream, exactly like everyone else. But when the conference ended, I knew I had to act. So I phoned three friends. They are chairmen of banks in New York, Paris, and Tokyo. They of course know about the dreamers. They heard me out. The ridicule I expected did not come. Instead, all three told me they had been wondering about the same thing. The governments won't act. They're tied up with voters and fear of losing power. Either the banks do this or it won't happen. My three friends immediately called three other allies in the financial world. These called three more. Within an hour, the group was formed. I've been waiting—"

He stopped at the sound of knocking. His secretary opened the door and said, "Sorry to disturb you, sir. But you told me to let you know the instant one of those gentlemen called."

"You did right, Mildred."

"Mr. Takayama is on line three."

"Thank you." He lifted the receiver, punched the button, and said, "Tenning here."

His delight shone from his eyes and his smile. "Wonderful news. Just wonderful."

He hung up the phone and said, "It's done."

20

─────◦◦◦─────

Reed was waiting by his car when Elena emerged from the SuenaMed headquarters. She left her SUV in the company lot, choosing instead to ride back to Melbourne with Reed. Elena had no idea how she would get home from her afternoon class, and just then she did not care. From the road she phoned Jacob, who was at Orlando Airport, waiting to board his flight. She told him about the meeting in Trevor Tenning's office. When she was done, the silence stretched out like the sunlit expressway connecting Orlando to the coast. Finally Jacob said, "You still want to go ahead with your plan?"

"Now more than ever," Elena replied. A tiny knot burned at the center of her being. "Timing is crucial."

"I understand."

"We need to assume there are only two days left," Elena went on. "Which means we need to begin our work immediately."

"You sound so certain. It seems to me the dream pattern has been broken."

"If the others have the same dream tonight as Trevor, the pattern is restored."

Jacob wanted to argue further, but Elena disengaged and ended the call. She was done talking.

At the hour Reed turned on the radio and found a news channel. They listened in silence as the newscaster read the lead story. A new entity called One World Bank had submitted a bid to rescue the ailing New England Bank. The group was also reportedly taking actions to restore calm within the turbulent European markets. There were few details. One World Bank's spokeswoman addressed the journalists with a heavy East Asian accent. When pressed, she said only that there would be plenty of time for particulars when the crisis had passed.

When the newscaster began a recap of that morning's press conference, Elena reached over and turned it off.

Reed let a few miles roll past in silence before saying, "One World Bank. That's uncomfortably close to a one world government."

Elena did not respond.

"Some folks might even say in today's world a single unified finance group would be a fair match to the warnings in the Book of Revelation." He drummed two fingers on the wheel. "Especially if this group does what Tenning described happened in his dream, setting up a single currency. Forget the legal issues involved in all this. The crisis is so serious the governments closest to catastrophe could fall over themselves, signing on to whatever will save their political skin."

Elena felt the coal burning more fiercely at the base of her gut and did not speak.

"If you were looking for a reason to manipulate dreams, I'd say world domination of the financial markets is a pretty solid motive."

Elena stared at the Florida-flat highway. She felt her own steam rise to join with the storm looming over the eastern horizon.

Reed went on, "Say the group has actually been in place for months. They are made up of banks whose combined power is enough to rock the markets and topple governments. Their wings were clipped by the recent economic crisis. They see laws being put in place that rein in their ability to do whatever they want, whenever they please. They're looking for a way to strengthen their hand, solidify their hold on international power." Reed glanced over. "Feel free to chime in at any point here."

"You're pulling the thoughts straight from my own head," Elena said.

"Say it's real. Say they're actually close to pulling off the scam of the millennium." Reed shook his head at the prospect. "What on earth do we do?"

Elena turned in her seat so that her entire body was focused on him and not all the storms and uncertainties beyond their protected compartment. She felt anger pulse through her. "There's no 'if' about this. They're doing it. We can't prove it. Yet. But we need to assume that it's happening. They planned this meticulously. They brought me in because of my reputation in dream analysis. They convinced me it was all real by instilling the dreams inside my head. They made me the spokesperson. They *used* me."

Reed slowed and looked over. His features were intensely grave as he repeated, "What do we do?"

"We pray. We plan. We act," Elena replied. "And we bring them down."

21

————————⬥————————

Thirty minutes into Elena's afternoon class, Reed Thompson's assistant walked down the classroom's center aisle with a note from Reed asking her to join him in the philosophy department as soon as her class was over. Elena thanked Reed's aide, slipped the note into her pocket, and resumed her lesson. She loved these hours with the students, now more than ever. Their energy was invigorating. Teaching was the one thing that separated her fully from the gathering tempest.

Her progress from the classroom was slowed by a gaggle of students who blocked the exit. The young woman who had requested her autograph after the first class asked, "Can we have a minute, Dr. Burroughs?"

"I'm due at a meeting with Dr. Thompson. Sorry."

The girl simply nodded and continued to block the aisle. "It's just, we wanted to know if you were a believer."

Elena searched her mind for a name to fit the face. She had always had a facility for names. But the past few days had taken their toll. Finally it came to her. "Brenda, isn't it?"

"Yes, ma'am."

"Brenda Twyford. Third-year pre-med major." Elena recited the facts mostly to show she was genuinely connected to Brenda and to this moment. "The answer to your question, Brenda, is yes. I believe, and I ask our Lord daily to help with my unbelief."

"Cool. I mean, we just wanted you to know, we'll be praying for you. All of us. Every day. It's a promise."

Elena felt her heart swell, and resisted the urge to hug the young lady. It would not help matters to burst into tears. "Thank you all. So much. Now I really must be going."

The glow carried her out of the building and into the afternoon's sultry heat. Yet another storm had come and gone. The wind carried a bayou quality of thick humidity and tropical fragrances. Elena was midway down the connecting sidewalk when the idea came to her, as though the young woman's words illuminated some recess of her mind. She slowed, and when the philosophy building's entrance came into view, she stopped altogether. She turned away from a group of approaching students and their whispered comments. She focused on a palm wilting in the heat and tried to draw the mental strands into some form of cohesive order. She gave it ten more minutes, long enough for the perspiration to stain her shirt. Then she allowed the pressure of the next step to move her forward.

The ACU campus underwent a drastic change beyond the new student center. The philosophy department occupied the first of a cluster of buildings dating from the sixties. The two-storied structure had old-fashioned louvered windows and low ceilings and an air conditioner that rattled and grumbled. The department was slated to move into new offices at the end of September. Or rather, they were moving if the hurricane did not strike.

The department secretaries were corralled into a glass-fronted structure opposite a useless waiting area, as if the building had been originally designed as a dentist's office. One of the staffers waved Elena into the room beyond their chamber. She knocked on the closed door and entered an empty classroom whose tables had been clustered into a conference shape. Reed Thompson stopped his pacing in front of the board and said, "Finally."

"I'm sorry to keep you waiting. I've had, well . . ."

"Another idea?"

"Half an idea. Maybe. That's why I was late. I wanted to give it time to germinate."

"Okay. I'm happy to talk it through if you think that might help, but first we need to do this." He slipped into a chair by a laptop. "The gentleman's name is Dr. Dwight Chester. Heard of him, by any chance?"

"Sorry. No."

"No reason you should. Dwight is assistant director of the FDA. He is absolutely to be trusted. Five years ago, he backed the wrong candidate for president and was slated for dismissal. I fought a hard battle to keep the man in place. He owes me. Not his life. But close."

"Why are we meeting here, Reed?"

"There's no way I can sweep my office or home for bugs without alerting watchers. If they're out there. Any discussion of evidence needs to take place in conditions like this."

Elena did as she was told. "Thank you, Reed. For backing my plans. This means the world."

"You're welcome, Elena. Now draw the blinds, please." His attention remained held by the computer and the sheet of handwritten instructions unfolded beside the laptop. "If anyone points a directional mike at a glass window, blinds will block their ability to overhear."

The laptop was decorated with a plastic rainbow and three sparkling flowers. "Is that Stacy's?"

"She said to tell you that she is praying for us. She also told me this would be easy to set up. I should . . ." The laptop chimed. "Okay, Dwight, are you there?"

"You're late, Reed. And I'm facing an extremely tight schedule."

Reed frowned across the table. Elena nodded agreement. The man sounded anything but cordial. "Sorry for the delay."

"Look, I've got to tell you, this is not a good place you've put me in. I know I owe you. But if I talked this over with my lawyers, they'd tell me I was well over the line even getting on the phone with you."

Reed's tone hardened to match the unseen man on the other end of the line. "I told you this was highly confidential."

"I didn't say I'd gone to legal. I just . . ." Dwight Chester sighed. "Look. The regulations governing our new product analysis are there for a reason. We are given exclusive access to highly confidential data. Divulging this information could literally bring down a company. What you're asking could mean a felony charge."

"I understand." Reed scribbled hastily at the bottom of his instruction sheet, then swiveled it around so Elena could read: *Dwight is not alone.*

"I really must insist on knowing what is going on and why you've approached me," Chester went on. "I have to warn you. If I don't like what I hear, I won't tell you a thing. Debts can only take you so far, Reed. You didn't break the law to help me."

"No. All I did was save a friend from professional ruin, and put my own job on the line to do so."

Dwight's voice trembled with the strain, but he held his ground. "I would hardly be a decent professional if I broke our code of ethics, much less the law."

Reed looked at Elena and silently mouthed two words. *Your call.*

Elena rose from her seat, rounded the table, and pulled out the chair next to Reed's. "Dr. Chester, my name is Dr. Elena Burroughs. I'm a clinical psychologist, with a particular focus on dream analysis. For the past week—"

"Wait, I know you. You're that woman on the news conferences. About the crisis."

"That is correct. And this is why I'm calling."

"But the drug Reed called me about, SuenaMed's new product, it's for the treatment of ADHD."

"And if that is all it does, then we have no further interest in the matter." Elena took a long breath. "Dr. Chester, what I'm about to tell you is extremely confidential. If any word of this conversation leaks out, I could be killed."

There was a silence, then, "Reed, is she on the level?"

"The answer is definitely yes. And both of us are potentially facing the most extreme risks," Reed said.

"In that case, the best assurance I can give you is what I said at the beginning of this conversation," Dwight Chester replied. "We are in the business of keeping secrets."

Elena said, "Recently we have been alerted to the possibility that this entire sequence of events is a scam."

"What, the dreams?"

"The dreams, the crisis, everything."

"How is that possible?"

"That is why I'm calling. We need further evidence. This requires our investigating two different directions, and doing so with all possible speed. Have you heard about the latest dream?"

"Two days," Dwight replied. "It gave me chills."

"One direction has to do with uncovering how this dream manipulation might have occurred. If it happened at all. SuenaMed has been at the heart of these events from the beginning. This is why I asked Reed to call. I have just two questions. First, would you please review the clinical trials related to SuenaMed's new drug to see if there is any hypnotic quality, anything that suggests it might carry the power of altering the patient's dream state. And second, is there perhaps another of SuenaMed's products that has shown such psychotropic qualities? We are looking for something that could be secretly administered, something that leaves no trail whatsoever."

There was a long pause, then the director asked, "You said your investigations were taking two directions. What is the other one?"

"We need to determine whether there is evidence of financial market manipulation."

Dwight's tone grew more worried still. "If you're talking about somebody big enough to rig international markets and topple governments, this would have to be somebody a lot bigger than SuenaMed."

"We agree."

"Any group that big, they'd have all the power in the world to cover their tracks. That is, if they exist."

Reed said, "Which is why we're taking such precautions."

Elena added, "We are trying as hard as we possibly can to identify the group without alerting them to our search. Your help could be vital."

"Okay. Give me fifteen minutes, then call me back."

When Reed cut the connection, he said, "Dwight is correct. Our chances of uncovering evidence are almost nil. Especially given the time constraints."

The idea she had first sensed on the pathway grew into crystal clarity. "Can we set up a safe call with Agatha Hune?"

"Of course. But if she had such evidence, don't you think . . ." His gaze tightened. "It's the next part of your idea, isn't it?"

She nodded slowly. "I think I may have found a way around that particular mountain."

Fifteen minutes later, Dr. Chester resumed the call by saying, "The FDA approval process for new prescription drugs follows a very concrete series of stages. Following the preliminary lab studies, all new drugs undergo extensive animal trials before being administered to human patients. These patients are carefully monitored, and all results must be divulged to the FDA committee responsible—"

Reed broke in: "Dwight, we are chasing shadows. We need the ninety-second version."

"Right." There was the sound of shuffling papers. "Suena-Med's new product is going into worldwide release next week under the name of SuenaMind. Or it will, if the economy doesn't explode in our faces. SuenaMind is a revolutionary new method of ADHD treatment. It is delivered as a nasal spray, administered once every two weeks."

"The timing works," Elena said to herself.

"Excuse me?"

"This entire sequence of dreams could fit within the time frame of one dose."

"But there is nothing in the experimental evidence to suggest it can affect the dream patterns of patients," Dwight said.

Reed demanded, "You are sure of this?"

"This is what I do. The clinical trials for SuenaMind are totally clean. No known side effects. Excellent short- and long-term results."

Reed gave her a long look, disappointment etched into his features. "This is not what we had hoped to hear."

"Sorry. But I have to tell you, this is as clean a study as I've ever seen." There was the sound of more papers being shifted. "The only thing that is even the least bit curious is how long it's taken SuenaMed to bring the drug on line."

"Explain what that means, please."

"We were alerted to this product's potential eight years ago. That's part of the FDA approval process. The instant a drug moves from lab work to animal testing, we are notified. Normally it would go from there to first human trials in about a year, perhaps two. SuenaMind took seven. Seven years would generally indicate there was a serious flaw, one that sent them back to the labs. In this case, four years ago SuenaMed's director of clinical trials died suddenly. We were notified that the final report would be delayed. That was the last we heard from them for, let's see . . ."

There came more sounds of pages being turned. "It was eleven months before they responded. Then a new product director was brought in. I have the letter of notification here in front of me."

"Rachel Lamprey," Elena said, her voice hollow.

"That's the lady. We immediately lodged a second official query with her. This is standard ops. Sometimes a delay means the drug company has reformulated the product to overcome side effects that emerged in the animal testing phase. But the lab results were clean, so I have no idea what happened here. In any case, Ms. Lamprey's new team was already moving at lightning speed. Within four months of her coming on board, the group filed their initial clinical trial report and moved into large-scale trials. As soon as these reports began confirming what the preliminary results had shown, their PR team started the first round of promotions, getting the medical community hungry for the product. Eight months ago, the initial license was issued. The rest you probably know. We have received notice from two other companies that they're working on their own products, but this is normal with any drug that has the potential of reshaping the market. Which this one does. SuenaMind will have the field to itself for at least two years, possibly three. Their profit potential is huge—we're talking billions."

Elena shook her head. This was not what she needed to know. She searched hard.

"You still there?"

"We're here," Elena replied. "Dr. Chester, one final question. Do you have any idea how the original team director died?"

"Sure, I can tell you precisely. The companies are required to file all such reports, in case we learn at a future date that the demise may be related to chemical exposure. Here it is. He died of a seizure that led to heart failure. The autopsy report suggested a latent epilepsy."

"Thank you, Dr. Chester."

"About your other question. SuenaMed does no research in psychotropics. Never has. Sorry I couldn't be of any more help."

Elena was already reaching to cut off the laptop. "This is exactly what we needed. Good-bye."

Reed eyed her doubtfully. "Really? It sounded like a total failure to me."

"Just the opposite." Elena reached for the instruction sheet, flipped it over, and began making notes. "I need to talk with Agatha Hune. Now. There isn't a moment to lose."

22

When the Federal Reserve bank executive came on the line, she said, "I'm glad you set up this call. I needed to speak with you as well."

Elena asked, "Are we secure at your end?"

"This is the phone for a café in the ground floor of my building."

"Reed says we shouldn't use any phone a second time."

"This is the man who called earlier on my private line, yes? Do I recognize his name?"

"Reed Thompson was formerly chief of the White House Council of Economic Advisers."

"Of course. He believes the threat is real?"

"More with every passing hour."

Agatha Hune released a breath. In the background came the clatter of dishes. "That is very reassuring."

"Can you run a check through official channels without it coming back to you?"

There was a moment's pause, then, "Theoretically, yes."

"We need to know if there have been any unexplained deaths

over the past two or three weeks within the ranks of senior international bank executives."

"You need to be more specific. What banks?"

"I have no idea. Big. Regional powerhouses."

"Any specific symptoms I should be looking for?"

"Unexplained seizures. Heart failure. Possibly diagnosed as an epileptic attack."

There was a pause, then, "Like the dreamer in France."

"That's right."

"Drug related?"

"If we're right, autopsy and blood work will have come back clean."

"Other than establishing a pattern, why is this important? Vague evidence will only take us so far, and the clock is ticking."

"If this is a scam where dream manipulation plays a role, we are talking about a drug whose impact on the patient is so powerful it dominates their most basic subconscious urges. It would be logical to assume, well . . ."

"They could also induce deadly seizures."

Elena fought down the stomach-churning queasiness. "We need to hurry."

"I am all too aware of the time pressure. Are you done at your end?"

"Yes."

"Because I have an issue of my own."

"I thought you might."

"Jacob Rawlings wants to hypnotize me. Apparently on your instructions."

"That's correct."

"I dislike the idea intensely. Especially given everything else that is happening. It smacks of just more mental exploitation."

"Jacob will give you very specific instructions. All to do with

supplying us with crucial evidence. He will instruct you to override other commands and *remember*."

Agatha was silent.

Elena went on, "If SuenaMed is manipulating our dream
states, they must begin with commands to forget we have been
told anything. There also has to be something they use as a trig-
ger. I have these vague recollections of a faceless messenger at
my door."

Agatha spoke very slowly. "All I remember is the ringing of a
phone and the feeling of terrible dread. I don't want to pick it up.
But I must."

Elena recalled the dismay and the powerlessness she had felt
as she had approached the door and the messenger. "It's highly
unlikely we can override something this forceful. So we're trying
to do the next best thing."

Agatha's voice carried the deep tremor of a strong woman
brought to the brink. "I'm so frightened."

"I understand. So am I." Elena fought a second surge of
nausea. "But if it's any consolation, I'm going to undergo hypnosis
as well."

The inland waterway was caught in the vise of another tropical
deluge as Elena crossed the causeway bridge in Reed's car. But as
she entered the barrier island and turned onto the road leading
north along the bayside, the pounding of rain on the car's roof
abruptly ceased. The effect was as gentle as it was jarring. To her
left, the inland waterway was lost behind a dark curtain. The rain
fell with such force that she could hear the constant hiss through
her closed window. To her right, the fading light of day illuminated a world of brilliant hues. Water cascaded from every roof,
every leaf. The air was impossibly clear. She rolled down her
window and savored the humid rush of fragrances.

The church parking lot was almost empty. Elena locked Reed's car and followed his directions to the church offices. Bob Meadows, Jacob's former roommate, was waiting for her in the lobby. Elena greeted him, then told the receptionist that Reed Thompson had called. The woman smiled, assured them everything was arranged, and led them down to an empty office.

When Elena had shut the door, she said, "Sorry about the subterfuge."

"I'm still having nightmares over getting shot at." His pudgy chin wavered slightly as he tried for a smile. "How are you, Elena?"

"Pressured. Worried. But calm." She imagined her own smile was hardly more genuine. "That probably sounds schizophrenic."

"It sounds like a woman holding up under intense pressure."

"I am. Both the pressure and the holding up," she confirmed. "Thanks to the prayers of a lot of good people."

"How do you want to do this?"

"To be honest, I've never been hypnotized before."

"I have a good deal of experience, as I told you on the phone. I find hypnosis can be useful in dealing with certain issues. Why don't you sit on the sofa there, in case you feel a need to lie down." He pulled over a chair. "I was not able to convince Senator Suarez to participate. Hardly a surprise. His character is defined by maintaining control."

"Which is no doubt why these experiences have left him perpetually angry."

This time his smile came easier. "It would hardly be professional of me to say that a certain patient has been angry since birth. Are you comfortable?"

"Yes. Thank you for coming."

"To be honest, I haven't been able to get you out of my mind. I was happy you asked. It's good to be able to do more." He pushed the coffee table to one side and pulled his chair in closer. "Though I was surprised you didn't ask Jacob."

"He needed to get back to Atlanta."

"Yes. So he said." He extracted a gold watch from his pocket. "He also said you had taken up with another gentleman. Jacob actually sounded jealous."

"A pocket watch? Are you serious?"

"The tried and true works best sometimes. And you have just changed the subject."

"When I was in Atlanta, I asked Jacob to pray with me. He refused."

"A world of answers in those simple words." Bob shook his head. "Jacob has spent his whole life fighting to have his way. This entire episode has been harder on him than you can possibly imagine."

Elena heard the man's apologetic tone, and said, "You are a good friend, Bob."

"I try to be."

"I'm sorry for all the trouble we've caused you. But I'm glad Jacob brought you into this."

"I'm glad too. Very glad. I mean that sincerely." He wound the watch in slow, smooth motions. As he did, the engraved gold face caught the light and flickered in Elena's eyes. "It's remarkable how much has been packed into the past few days, isn't it? So many things to work through. It makes you so very tired, doesn't it? I imagine you would like to just set all those thoughts and concerns aside for a while. And the travel, down to Miami and up to Atlanta and to and from the university where you teach. You're still teaching, aren't you, Elena?"

"Yes. And there's Orlando." She felt as though her tongue was thickening, making the words hard to form.

"Orlando, of course. So much travel. And so many thoughts. All of them whirring about, leaving you so tired at times. There's nothing you'd like more than to set all these thoughts and concerns aside, and just relax, relax, relax . . ."

Elena wanted to tell him that the watch was spinning so hard he was going to drop it. But suddenly she was unable to shape the thoughts, much less the words.

23

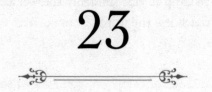

The retired female police officer settled herself comfortably on Elena's screened porch. "Great view."

Reed had told Elena that the woman had been in the Sunday school class, but she did not remember her. "I can't thank you enough for coming."

"I've been watching the evening news and feeling more helpless than I have since my husband became ill that last time. It's good to have a role to play."

Dorothy was in her late sixties and heavyset in the manner of a woman who valued her own strength. Elena found her presence very reassuring. "I'm afraid you're in for a very boring night."

"I've been on more stakeouts than you've had hot dinners." She pulled knitting needles and yarn from her bag. "You just go get ready for bed."

"You know where the tea and cups are."

"I'll be fine." The needles clicked a moment. "Those bodyguards hovering around the entrance to your complex, they're yours?"

"They are assigned to me, but by other people."

"Are they part of the problem?"

"I wish I knew."

Dorothy nodded, as though she had expected nothing less. "You go get some sleep. Nobody's getting in here tonight."

The dream came soon after she shut her eyes, or so it seemed the next morning. The sensation Elena carried from sleep was as strong as after every other dream. But this morning there was no dread. No screams that sawed at the pre-dawn light. Only bliss.

The problem was, the hypnosis had not worked. Elena recalled nothing whatsoever. Nothing, that is, except the dream itself.

She lay and stared at the ceiling and felt new tendrils of doubt swirl about her. What if the dreams were genuine? What if she and the other dreamers shared real moments of foretelling? What if they had somehow managed to pierce the veil of now? What if her entire investigation was not merely wrong, but dangerous? What if the divine hand was truly at work, and she was the one seeking to wrest control back to a human level? What if God did not respond to her prayers because he had already said everything he intended?

When she emerged from the bedroom, the retired police officer stood in the kitchen alcove. "Coffee?"

"Yes, thank you." Seldom had the fresh-brewed coffee aroma smelled better.

Dorothy handed Elena a mug. "Everything was quiet out here."

Elena poured milk from the little pitcher. The fog resulting from the dream might have been more pleasant than on other such mornings. But the sense of disconnect was just the same, if not stronger. Elena stared across the living room and out past the screened porch to where the water sparkled. The dream seemed more real than her own kitchen. "Thank you again. For being here."

"No problem." Dorothy refreshed her own mug. "The only thing stirring last night was you."

Elena paused with the mug halfway to her mouth. "Excuse me?"

Dorothy asked, "Do you sleepwalk?"

The words created a jarring discord in her brain. "I'm sorry, what?"

"You're right. It's none of my business."

"No, that's not . . ." Elena drank from the mug, set it down, and used both hands to rub her face. "Why would you ask if I sleepwalk?"

"Well, you popped up about an hour after you lay down. I thought maybe you'd heard something. I called out, but you didn't respond."

"I don't remember any of that."

"No, I guess you wouldn't. Don't suppose you remember picking your phone up off the table by the lamp there and carrying it into the bathroom."

"I . . . What?" Elena excused herself and padded back into the bathroom. There it was, her cell phone set on the little ledge above the sink. She picked it up, turned it on, and drew up the last number dialed. The screen was blank. It showed no numbers at all. Elena did not have a landline. She used this phone all the time. But the screen showed nothing. She tried to remember if this had happened before. But her mind seemed incapable of focusing.

Reed Thompson drove her into Orlando. He waved aside her concern over his missed appointments and did not speak as she described the dream and the phone and the lingering sense of disconnect.

When she had finished, Elena asked, "Is that possible? Can you sweep a phone's memory clean?"

"If you're asking, could I personally do it, the answer is definitely not. I have trouble switching mine on."

"Could anyone?"

"Theoretically, outsiders can do just about anything except make a phone stand up and bark. Just before the Beijing Olympics, the Chinese perfected a new parasite software that rode a cell phone signal into any phone and turned it into a locator beacon. Since then, new programs have been designed to alert a secret listener every time the phone makes a call. It also sends a duplicate text message to a third party."

Elena continued to rub her face, trying to press her brain into a semblance of alertness. "My head feels scrambled."

"Can hypnotism do that?"

Even trying to remember her professional studies was a trial. "Not in principal."

"But if the hypnotic orders seek to override something more deeply embedded, something stronger, what then?"

"I suppose . . . it might make the subject feel exactly as I do."

"So let's just review what we know."

"We don't *know* anything at all," Elena groaned. "And that's the problem."

"Bear with me a minute. Say some unknown enemy uses the phone to send instructions, tell the dreamer what to experience. And at the end of that call, they give instructions about the next time."

"The *next* time."

"Right. They say when the subject needs to call them back. This means even if the dreamers are shielded by guards and have family sleeping in the bed with them, the enemy can still reprogram the dream state when and where they want." Reed shook his head. "I have to tell you, it's diabolical, but it's brilliant."

"What if we're wrong? What if these dreams are a genuine warning from beyond?"

Reed looked over. "When we spoke this morning, I asked how you felt. Remember what you said?"

"Blissfully happy. And extremely sad."

"To my mind, that's all the warning I need. You have an external source that is seeking to implant an emotional state. And a deeper source, a *real* source, that is telling you what you *actually* feel."

"How can you be so certain?"

"Elena, there is nothing about this entire scenario that corresponds to what the Scriptures tell us." Reed bunched one fist and softly struck the wheel in time to his words. "That is the key. That is the one eternal, unchanging element by which we must judge everything that life throws at us. Including this."

She reached over and took hold of the fist. At her touch, his fingers unfolded and intertwined with hers. "Thank you for being here for me. So much."

Elena shut her eyes and leaned her head against the seat back, willing herself to do whatever it took to push the night away and focus. After a time, Reed turned on the news channel. Two stories dominated the airwaves. Overnight the One World Bank concept had apparently caught fire. The same spokeswoman with her solemn tone and strong East Asian accent talked of a need for a unified response to avert the global catastrophe.

These same words were repeated by several foreign leaders, then altered slightly and mouthed by two members of Congress. Three Wall Street executives trumpeted their own versions. Pundits dissected the latest developments with ecstatic relief. The roiling markets appeared to have calmed somewhat. Portugal was apparently being dragged back from the brink of national insolvency. The New England Bank announced it would reopen its doors the next day. Gold had retreated almost two hundred dollars an ounce from its latest stratospheric high. The newscaster finished the story with the statement that yet another announcement was soon expected from the Orlando dreamers. The dreamers had become the oracle of the crisis. The world awaited whatever it was they had to say. That was fact.

The other news story was the hurricane. Hector was its name, a category four, with winds touching a hundred and thirty miles an hour, larger now than the state of Texas. The newscaster described the havoc Hector had left in its wake after brushing against the Dominican Republic. Half of the hurricane watchers and their computer models showed Hector taking aim at Cape Canaveral, which meant that in three days Melbourne would be directly in the eye of the storm. The other computer models showed it moving off to sea, bypassing land entirely. Elena wished she could feel more concern, but just then she had room only for the tempest surrounding her.

Elena did not open her eyes again until her phone rang. When she saw who it was, she answered, "Good morning, Jacob."

"How was your night?"

"Jarring. But pleasant." They had agreed to be cryptic in all such open conversations. She imagined her tone was as flat and distant as his. "Agatha had the dream?"

"She did, yes." He paused. "She's found it very difficult to concentrate this morning."

"I feel the same."

"Nothing else to report from this end," Jacob went on. "Sorry."

"No. It's the same here." A few images flashed through the morning glare. A memory wavered in the heat. Something she had not recalled before just then. But she could not draw it into focus. It was like trying to read a book through the waters of a rushing stream.

"Elena?"

"Yes, I'm here."

"Agatha says she'll be in touch as soon as she has something to report. In the meantime, she asked me to tell you that she is more certain than ever. Despite everything to the contrary."

Elena breathed a sigh of pure relief. "Thank you both."

The SuenaMed headquarters loomed ahead of them, a molten image of commercial might. Elena squinted against the glare and the fear that filled her. "I don't want to do this."

"I don't blame you."

"But I have to." She looked at Reed, hoping against hope. "Don't I?"

"The only way we can buy the necessary time is by your acting as close to normal as—"

"Nothing about this entire process is normal. The whole experience *defies* normal."

Reed's only response was to reach over and take her hand.

"I can't be their spokesperson. I just can't."

"I understand."

"But they'll be expecting it."

"Here's what we're going to do. We'll pray. Then you'll go in there, knowing God will guide your steps. And you will listen for his guidance. And you will do his will."

"But what if . . ."

He waited until he was certain she would leave the rest of her fear unspoken. "Let's bow our heads."

24

⎯⎯⎯⎯⎯⎯⎯⎯⎯⎯

Perhaps it should have felt odd, entering what increasingly appeared to be the enemy's lair, with neither weapon nor protection, not even her phone. Not to mention the gaggle of late-arriving reporters who tried to confront her in the lobby. She would have been mauled, except a guard rushed over. The stocky man inserted himself between Elena and the yammering reporters. He was swiftly joined by Reginald, who ushered her toward the elevators while rudely shoving the reporters away.

But all Elena could think of, as the elevator doors shut on the lobby and the din, was how much she just wanted to be certain. About the direction she was taking. About the threat. About the nation and the economy. About what God wanted her to do.

She realized Reginald had said something to her. Elena replied, "I want you to call off your bodyguards."

"Dr. Burroughs, I'm not sure . . ." He stopped as the doors opened.

"I want them gone," she said firmly, and strode away.

To her vast relief, the dreamers' conference call was cut short. Several of the major television networks begged them to start the news conference early, as they wanted to carry the conference live before the markets opened. As she was rushed down the main corridor and into the jammed conference hall, Elena struggled for some way of telling a tight-lipped Rachel and the others that she would not be their spokesperson any longer. Every seat was taken. The lights from the television crews were blinding.

Then the conference room door opened, and Trevor Tenning entered. The CEO of SuenaMed wore an ethereal smile as he walked over and said, "You had the dream."

"I did. Yes."

"It shows." His face appeared to almost glow. "It came to me again last night as well. Is there any reason why I should have had it a day early?"

"I don't . . . I can't say."

"I understand." He slipped into the chair next to hers and nodded a greeting to the others. "Perhaps the intention was for me to help save the bank while there was still time."

"I . . . Perhaps."

"Or maybe it was to emphasize a different need." He drummed his fingers on the table, as though in deep thought. "Perhaps it is time for me to become the face before the world."

Elena nodded slowly, watching him closely.

"You have done a remarkable job as spokesperson for our group. But I am just wondering if perhaps this was the reason why I had this dream before all the others. So that I might prepare myself for this moment."

She knew he wanted to sound thoughtful. As though he were still working through all this in his head. But the words carried a rehearsed quality.

Elena rose from her chair and moved over to stand by the side wall next to Rachel.

This time, Trevor Tenning's reaction was genuine. "I didn't mean to supplant you, Dr. Burroughs."

She waved for him to begin. "I'm fine right here."

Elena slipped from the room as the news conference drew to a close. She was the first out the door. The corridor was empty. It was so quiet she could hear a computer terminal in an office she passed, tuned to an online news channel, playing a live feed of Trevor Tenning's final remarks. Over a dozen people crowded into the office, listening to their CEO. They were totally silent, engrossed in what they assumed was the unfolding of an economic lifeline.

The elevator was glitzy in a slick corporate fashion, with polished bronze walls and a small flat screen embedded above the controls. The face of Trevor Tenning filled the screen. The sound was too low for Elena to make out his words, but she knew what he was saying. Trevor Tenning had spent three-quarters of an hour reshaping the same simple message. He was polished, adroit, and showing his worldwide audience a calming yet authoritative demeanor.

If she did not know better, Elena would have thought Trevor Tenning was born for this day and this role.

Elena crossed the lobby and was almost to the exit when one of the dark-jacketed guards called from the receptionist station, "Dr. Burroughs, wait, just a second."

She did not stop or turn around. "What is it?"

"You're wanted back upstairs."

"Sorry. That's not possible. I have to—" She let the doors close behind her, sealing off words she had no intention of saying.

The heat and thick humidity were a welcome change. She took deep drafts of the cloying air, as though she had spent the previous two hours holding her breath.

Reed pushed the passenger door open and called, "How did it go?"

"Fine. It was fine. Can we leave?"

He pulled away from the curb. On the radio a newscaster was recapping the interview. Elena reached over and cut it off.

Reed said, "You didn't have to speak."

"No." She picked up her phone from the center console. "Have they called?"

"Not yet." He stopped for a light and glanced over. "Elena . . ."

"What?"

"Nothing."

"Say it, Reed. Please."

The light changed, and he started forward. "When the pressures are strongest and the harsh winds blow, it is hard to stop and accept that we've been visited by, well . . ."

She nodded slowly, and said softly to the sun-splashed window, "Miracles."

Almost in response, her phone rang. She checked the readout and said, "It's Rachel."

"He was with you then, and he is with you now," Reed said. "Count on it."

When Elena opened the connection, Rachel launched straight in. "What on earth are you doing?"

"Driving home."

"Don't you realize how vital your presence is just now?"

"Your Mr. Tenning seemed to be doing just fine."

"He isn't usurping your position, Elena."

"I never said—"

"You are the face the world associates with this phenomenon." Rachel paused, and when she spoke next, her voice had risen almost a full octave. "And what on *earth* is this about you dismissing the bodyguards we assigned?"

"I'm making other arrangements."

"They were placed there to *protect* you."

"What right do you have to question any of my actions?"

"I . . . We're concerned for your safety. Don't forget the attack in Miami."

"I'm not forgetting anything. This is my life, Rachel. It sounds to me like you're trying to seal me off, *control* me."

Rachel backed off a trace and tried for composure. "Obviously the pressure is getting to you. I would like to think your safety, the *world's* safety, is our first concern."

"I want your bodyguards out of my life." Elena cut the connection. There was really nothing more that could be said without jeopardizing everything. The unspoken doubts lingered on her tongue, like a foul scent that drifted in from the wetlands beyond the highway. Her late best friend's sister. A traitor to everything Elena and Miriam both held dear.

Elena toyed with her phone. She was tempted to turn it off. Reed must have understood, for he said, "Best leave it on. We're still waiting to hear from the others."

She looked at him.

"What is it?"

"I was just thinking how grateful I am that you have been brought into my life," Elena said. "Thank you, friend."

Reed directed his words toward the front windshield. "I'd like to be more than that. Your friend, I mean."

She nodded slowly. "So would I."

"Really?"

"Yes, Reed. Really."

"Wow." His smile competed with the sunlight. "That's great, then."

Elena studied this good and strong man, and wished she could recapture the ability to smile with such abandon. "Yes, Reed. It surely is."

The phone remained silent until they exited the interstate, when Jacob rang. "Ah, I was wondering, well, when we could talk."

"Hang on and I'll ask." She held a swift consultation with Reed, then Elena asked, "Do you have a pen?"

"Yes, go ahead."

Elena repeated the number Reed fed to her. "We can be there in twenty minutes."

"Make it thirty. We may be joined by a couple of people."

Elena confirmed, then waited for Jacob to hang up. "Was there something else?"

"Is someone there with you?"

"Reed drove me to Orlando."

The handsome psychologist's sigh rattled the phone. "I hate how I've been relegated to the role of interested third party."

"Jacob, I want you to listen very carefully. Do you remember when we were together at CNN headquarters? What I said, the request I made?"

A pause, then, "I remember."

"You made a choice. One of life-altering importance."

"It always comes back to that, doesn't it?" He sounded petulant.

"Now and forever. And it's not too late to change your mind." She gave that a moment, then nodded to the sunlight and his silence. "We will expect your call."

"We've found our first concrete evidence."

The Federal Reserve bank executive's voice was almost metallic with tension. Elena and Reed sat on stools to either side of a speakerphone set on a lab bench. The empty room was in one of the older buildings that were slated for demolition. All of the classes and professors had been transferred over to the new structures. The air was sweltering. The lights still worked, but the AC was shut down. Elena could not have cared less. "Tell us."

"In the past three weeks, nine senior international financial executives have suffered seizures and heart failure," Agatha Hune reported. "Five of these occurred on the same night. No one put it together until now, because the victims are spread around the globe."

"They're tying up loose ends," Suarez said. "Doing away with people who might have opposed their plan."

"It's hardly the sort of evidence we can use to bring them down," Reed said.

"But it's a giant step in the right direction," Elena countered. "It's the first concrete evidence we have of a conspiracy."

"There's no way that many people disconnected by space and lifestyles could have naturally suffered the same effect in that short a time," Jacob agreed.

"There's something else." Elena related her conversation with the retired police officer, then said to Reed, "Tell them what you said on the way in this morning."

While Reed explained the concept of preprogramming dream-time instructions, Elena reviewed what they knew and what needed to come next. Which meant she was ready when Mario Suarez asked, "So what do we do now?"

"Trevor Tenning is the key," Elena replied. "We need to trace his roots and his current actions."

"And fast," Agatha added. "The international consortium of banks is firming up. We've just received word that the White House is preparing a statement. The consortium has formally entered into talks with the Fed to acquire two other ailing US banks. I've been called to Washington for a meeting of the Fed's board."

"I'm on it," Suarez said. "I'll be back to you this afternoon."

25

———✦———

Reed was locking the lab door when Elena's cell phone rang. She checked the readout. "I don't recognize the number."

"We can't risk missing something vital," he decided. "Answer it."

"This is Dr. Burroughs."

"Elena, it's Trevor Tenning."

"Yes, Mr. Tenning. How are you?"

"In quite a rush, as you can imagine. But a hundred percent better than yesterday. Rachel tells me you've elected to draw away from our group."

"That's reading a bit too much into it, sir." Elena moved in close enough for Reed to listen as well. "I simply needed to make some personal space. It looks as though this is going to drag on far longer than I anticipated. I don't feel comfortable having guards around me day and night."

"That is one point we can certainly agree on, though you may decide your safety requires them."

"Perhaps, but I doubt it. In the meanwhile, I'm being helped out by friends from my Sunday school."

"I see." He sounded extremely doubtful. "Are they professional?"

"Very." She could feel Reed's warmth compressed by their closeness and the room's confines. She took great comfort from him. "Was that why you called?"

"No, actually there was something else I wanted to discuss with you. It has to do with the vital role you have played in our group, and in this entire process. I wanted you to know that plans to form the consortium are moving forward. We are pressed by events to accelerate our actions on all fronts."

"So you are going to be a part of this?"

"We both are, if you accept my proposal. The consortium's board will be based on Wall Street. Which is where I'm headed as we speak. I'm actually phoning you from our jet. I have discussed this with the new board. We want you to join us."

"Excuse me?"

"We want to give you a seat on the board of the new international banking consortium. We haven't decided on a name yet, all such niggling details can wait. For the moment we're just calling it the One World Bank. We recognize the vital role you have played in all this. My fellow board members have agreed that you should also be granted one percent of the consortium's shares, which will grant legitimacy to your having a seat on the board."

"Trevor, Mr. Tenning . . . I don't know what to say."

Reed stepped away from her, slipped a pad and pen from his jacket, and scribbled hastily. Tenning went on, "All of the board is well aware of the power your dream analysis has had upon the shaping of this group. And of your ability to communicate with the public. We want you to remain as the consortium's official spokesperson. We can only assume your presence will continue to be invaluable."

Reed showed her the note, which read, *Yes is the only safe response.*

"Thank you," Elena said weakly. "I accept."

Four hours later, Suarez responded to Elena's news: "One percent of an international financial consortium is a huge bonus."

"The number of governments lining up to affirm this project is growing," Agatha Hune agreed. "The One World Bank's success is all but assured."

"We can't let that happen," Reed Thompson declared.

"Right now I don't see how we can stop it," Suarez responded.

"Much as I hate to admit defeat, we don't have enough to go public," Agatha agreed.

"So Elena accepts their offer and works at finding evidence from within," Suarez said. "And reaps a few million for her troubles."

"More like tens of millions," Agatha replied.

Elena and Reed and Jacob were gathered around the head of the psychology department's desk. Jacob had flown down in the afternoon, arriving just in time for the meeting. A staccato drumbeat of showers hammered the window. Lightning flashed brief silhouettes of a rain-swept world. Reed Thompson said, "If we wait, there is a chance of this consortium becoming so entrenched that whatever we deliver won't be enough to dislodge them."

"Much as I hate admitting it, I don't see that we have an alternative," Agatha replied.

Elena said, "Let's get back to the subject at hand. Tell us about Tenning."

"My staff has done a superb job," Suarez claimed. "Especially given the time pressure. The evidence is unmistakable. Trevor Tenning is the banks' man."

The three gathered around the cluttered desk exhaled a single breath. "Explain," Reed said.

"The trail is intended to mislead. But the signs are there. Trevor Tenning rose up through the ranks of a company that was acquired by one of the world's largest merger and acquisition firms. Following the corporate purchase, the new owners sent Tenning to head up another of their acquisitions. Then two things happened to disguise the trend. First, the buyout firm started operating through three overseas groups in which they had a controlling interest, thus masking their ownership. And second, they were themselves bought out by one of the world's largest banks."

Jacob asked, "This isn't enough to take public?"

"What we lack," Agatha replied, "is the smoking gun. Direct evidence of collusion. A clear indication that the banks manipulated both the economies and the minds of us dreamers."

"And had a hand in the demise of those executives who stood in their way," Reed added.

Elena asked, "How did Tenning become involved with SuenaMed?"

"According to the SEC records, three years ago a Paris bank acquired a nine percent stake in SuenaMed. This was a huge investment, and matched by a stake taken by a Japanese bank. Neither has any direct connection to Tenning, past or present. Two weeks after the filing, Tenning was named CEO."

Elena asked, "When, exactly?"

"Wait, I have it somewhere. Here it is. Four years and eleven days ago," Suarez replied.

"So only a few days after the product director for SuenaMind was murdered," Elena said.

There was a long silence, then Suarez said, "The thought of them getting away with this makes my blood boil."

26

As they were leaving the office, Jacob cleared his throat and said, "I was wondering if I could have a private word."

Reed frowned, but said, "If Jacob can drive you back to your home, I'll swing by and pick you up tomorrow."

Jacob asked, "Where is your car?"

"Still in the SuenaMed lot."

"I've booked a hotel room over on the island," Jacob said. "I can drive you into Orlando for the morning press conference. It's no trouble."

She saw the silent appeal in Jacob's gaze, and said, "All right."

Reed locked up the building's entrance, and together they ran through the pelting storm. He offered them a hasty farewell, then got into his car.

As Jacob turned out of the parking lot, he squinted against the downpour and asked, "How can you stand this weather?"

"I love it here," Elena replied. "Even with everything that's happened since I arrived, I feel like I have found a home."

"Hurricanes and all?"

"Yes, Jacob. Is the Florida weather what you wanted to discuss?"

"No." He turned onto the main road and headed toward the causeway bridge. "My father has an iron will. When I was growing up, his children were expected to be the smiling face of his own faith at work. There was no room for my questions or any personal direction that threatened this facade. I was glad to leave my faith behind. There, I've said it." He stared at the rain streaking the night-clad windshield for a time, then added, "But I miss the comfort of those early days."

"Does this mean you're willing to consider the possibility that God is at work here?"

"This is why I needed to talk with you. It's not just about the dreams. It's about how my entire scientific perspective has been turned on its head."

"I understand. Whether or not these dreams have been manipulated, you have found yourself realizing that your vision of the world, your personal construct, was not enough. Your own strength let you down when you needed it most. Even now, when it is becoming apparent that these dreams have been somehow implanted and all of us have been used as tools for their gain—"

"I cannot ignore the fact that I have needed answers beyond myself," he softly confirmed. "It has kept me up at night. The vacuum inside me. Seeing you and Reed in these moments, with your calm and your trust. I have observed you both, and I know the unseen is at work in you. Even when I tried my hardest to tell myself that it was all myth, that I was fooling myself."

"I am so grateful for your honesty, Jacob." As they left the bridge, Elena directed him onto the road leading to her condo. The world was a quiet wash of rain and empty streets and flickering streetlights. Elena pointed him toward her development, and he parked the car.

Jacob's face had grown cavernous from the effort of speaking. Her heart went out to him. But only so far. "I cannot tell you how beautiful it is to speak with you in this way. But whatever step you take now, it has to be for the right reason. Do you understand?"

His mouth opened, and he tasted a word. But no sound emerged.

"I have no idea what tomorrow holds. But if there is a chance, I want to build a life with Reed." She heard the love in her own voice, the soft hope, a song for the future she never thought would be hers to claim. "If you are doing this for me, it won't work. I'm sorry. But you need to understand this."

He stared at her a long moment, more than night shadows creasing his features. "You're sure?"

"Yes. I am."

He nodded slowly. "When I was boarding the flight, I had this sudden impression that I was traveling down for the wrong reasons. I felt . . . selfish. Ashamed. And I didn't understand why. Until now."

She reached over and took his hand. One friend offering solace to another. "Would you like to pray with me?"

27

Dorothy already had the kettle boiling when Elena entered her home. The retired policewoman had a no-nonsense solidity to her that Elena found very reassuring. "I didn't notice your bodyguards tonight."

"They've been dismissed."

"So it's just me on duty." She did not seem to mind that in the least.

Elena set a chamomile tea bag in her cup. She felt so tired her bones ached. Perhaps the tea would help calm her mind. But as she took her first sip, her phone rang. The readout said it was Rachel. Elena was very tempted not to answer. But the day looming beyond the night and the storm forced her hand. "Yes?"

"Why is it," Rachel demanded, "that you suddenly distrust me?"

Elena resisted the sudden surge of emotions. Perhaps it just fatigue. But she was certain she heard a vestige of Miriam's voice in those words. Angrily she pushed it all aside. She needed clarity and control now more than ever. "You already know the answer to that."

"No, no, you are incorrect, what you say." Rachel's voice had taken on a slight accent, as though the events and the pressures and the emotions had torn away her civilized and educated veneer. "I have done everything in my power to do right by you. I protected you every step of the way. Nothing has changed."

Elena carried the phone out onto the screened-in porch. The storm was passing now. Rain dripped lazily from her roof, while off in the distance lightning silhouetted mountains of clouds. "For the second time tonight, you're totally off course."

"I . . . What?"

"Everything . . . Wait a moment, please." Elena pressed the phone to her ribs and stared at the night. A thought had come to her, brilliant as the brief illuminations off to her right. She took a breath. Another. Trying to steady herself.

Reed would definitely not approve of what she was about to do. And yet, what alternative did they have? The reality had been stated during their telephone conference. If they waited, the new banking order would become entrenched. No matter what evidence they brought forward, it would be too late to turn things around.

It was either now or never.

Elena walked back into the condo. She asked Dorothy, "Can I use your phone?"

"No problem."

"Thanks." Elena stepped to the side table where she kept a pen and notepad. "Rachel, where are you calling from?"

"My office."

"Do you have a number where I can call you, one that isn't linked to you in any way?"

"Is this really necessary?"

"Yes. And it needs to be totally removed from any risk of a potential microphone catching your words."

"Wait a moment." The phone was set down. Then: "Call me back at this number."

Elena wrote it down, ended the call, then dialed the number into Dorothy's phone.

As soon as she came on the line, Rachel implored, "All I'm asking is for you to trust me."

"Prove you're worth it."

She was silent a moment. "What do you mean?"

"Do you really think there is nothing at all wrong with this situation? Either you were a part of it from the beginning, or you are blinded by your trust in Trevor Tenning."

"H-he gave me my big break. I was just another junior VP, and he appointed me head of this new division. He's mentored me since he first came on as CEO—"

"I know all that. And it changes nothing. There is something terribly wrong at SuenaMed. Either you help me, or you are one of them. The enemy."

Rachel was quiet for so long Elena thought she had cut the connection. A very different woman came back, subdued and afraid. "The economic crisis isn't real?"

"Of course it's real. That's not what I am saying, Rachel. It's also *manufactured*."

"By Trevor?"

"He is the public face, yes."

"I don't . . . You're . . ." Rachel faltered, stopped, breathed hard. "What do you mean?"

Elena reached out and traced the pattern of a raindrop on her window. Thunder rippled through the air, a powerful resonance of unseen forces at work. She was taking a terrible risk. But there was no time for discussion or argument or hunting down alternatives. Elena said, "Do you have access to the original research for SuenaMind?"

"Do I . . . You're not making any sense."

"Yes or no, Rachel."

"I am SuenaMind's product director. Of course I can access it. All the way back to the original molecular formulation."

"Not that far. I'm talking about the research leading up to the murder of your predecessor."

"That's not . . . He wasn't . . ."

"There was an unexpected medical discovery. One your company and its owners have kept secret. So you won't find anything in the corporate files. You'll need to access the former director's personal data. Maybe he hid disks somewhere, or a laptop, something."

There was a long silence, then, "What am I looking for?"

"We are working on a thesis that goes as follows: Under certain circumstances, your drug creates a hypnotic state so powerful it can dominate even the most basic subconscious urges. Including the formation of dream states. We need evidence to prove this is correct."

Rachel moaned softly. Perhaps in denial. Perhaps in dismay at what Elena had uncovered. "What brought you to this?"

"That's not your concern, Rachel." That was also the sort of question the enemy would be asking. Elena fought against the terror that threatened to swamp her. But she could do nothing about the metallic tone of her voice. "You want me to trust you? Then find me the evidence that confirms what we already know. Give us what we need to take this public. We have to stop them before it's too late. And Rachel."

The woman responded with a voice both ancient and deep. "Yes?"

"Don't call back unless you have what we need."

28

When Elena returned to her living room, Dorothy was seated at one of the breakfast stools, her knitting piled on the counter beside her mug. "Your tea's gone cold."

"I'll make another."

The television was on and showed an excited reporter being drenched by torrential rain and wind. Dorothy said, "The hurricane's moved over the southern islands of the Bahamas. Our own forecast is coming up. I'll cut it off if you want."

"No, it's fine." She poured out her mug and reheated the kettle. Over the breakfast counter she watched as the weather forecasters explained why Hector's path was still impossible to predict. A high-pressure zone over the Midwest states might or might not move eastward. The high-pressure zone was potent enough to hold the hurricane offshore. The weather forecaster was almost apologetic as he explained the difficulty they were having in predicting movement of both weather systems. Then the channel switched to an advertisement. Elena muted the sound and set Dorothy's cell phone and her own on the counter next to the policewoman's knitting. "I want you to do something for me."

"Why I'm here."

"Whatever happens, whatever I might say," Elena told her solemnly, "don't let me use any phone."

Elena slept and did not dream. Or rather, she dreamed and all of the dreams were her own.

She awoke to a remarkable sense of calm. The clock read a quarter to seven. She had not bothered to set the alarm because she had not expected to sleep so long or so well. Jacob was due to pick her up in just over an hour. If she hurried, she had time for a brief workout.

When Elena emerged from the bedroom in jogging shorts and T-shirt, Dorothy greeted her with a smile and a lifting of her coffee mug. "Good night?"

"The best. Nothing happened. What about from your end?"

"Your phone rang once. I answered, and they clicked off."

"Did you make note of the number?"

"Caller withheld. I called a pal on the force, they ran a check. Disposable phone assigned to one Mr. Jones."

Elena entered the kitchen and poured herself a mug. "A lie."

"Happens all the time. The salespeople will forgo the ID check for a ten-spot." The policewoman sipped again. "Do you recall our little conversation?"

"You mean, we talked last night?"

"You showed up. Sleepwalking again. Started across the living room, I assume for your phone. I told you to go back to bed. Said it a second time." Dorothy pointed into the living room with her mug. "You touched the place where you set down your phone. Sort of grabbed at it with your hand, then you turned and walked back into the bedroom."

Elena released a breath she had not realized she had been holding. "Thank you."

"Just doing my job." Dorothy refreshed both their mugs. "Sorry I can't run with you. Hip replacement."

"The development has a small gym. I can put in a half hour on the elliptical before Jacob gets here."

"I'll come down and keep watch." Dorothy spooned in half a sugar. "Jacob, that's the fellow who dropped you off?"

"Yes. Jacob Rawlings is a clinical psychologist from Atlanta."

"Smart and handsome both." She sipped and nodded approval. "There's some who'll tell you marrying into your profession only guarantees you'll take your work home. I married a cop. Good man. We had thirty-one great years before his heart went."

"I'm so sorry for your loss." She finished her mug and set it in the sink. "Jacob says he wants to be my beau. But he's not."

Dorothy liked that. "You got a thing against handsome men?"

"No, I . . ." Elena was almost grateful when the phone started ringing. "Is that one yours?"

"Believe so." Dorothy walked to her purse on the sofa, answered, listened a moment, then reentered the kitchen and said, "Your friend Rachel sounds in a bad way."

"She must have made note of your number when I called her last night." Elena started out onto her screened-in porch, then entered her bedroom and asked, "Are you calling from a safe place?"

"The basement of a man who died four years ago." Rachel's voice was both low and unsteady. "A man my company murdered."

Her relief at having taken a proper risk left her weak at the knees. Elena seated herself at the desk by the window and reached for a pad and pen. "Tell me everything."

. . . . .

Rachel spoke in fits and starts, interrupting herself to add details and to regain her fractured control. Her predecessor's name was Larry Kroom. He had started the search for a new ADHD treatment, and led it from day one. His motive was simple and very personal. Both of his children suffered from attention deficit hyperactivity disorder. Two boys. Identical twins. Eleven years old when they lost their father. At this point, Rachel had to stop and set down the phone. Elena listened to the woman try to stifle broken sobs, and knew with an expansive relief two great truths. First, they had the smoking gun. And second, Rachel Lamprey was on their side.

When she finally came back on the line, Rachel went on, "His wife said SuenaMed security came and cleaned out his office. But the records I'm holding weren't in his office. They were hidden in a box behind the children's infant clothes, at the back of a cluttered and dusty basement. On top was a note to his wife that said simply, 'Only give this to someone you can trust, and only if they ask for it.'" Rachel had great difficulty forming the word *trust*. As though just speaking it left her convicted of some vast wrong.

Larry Kroom had discovered the drug's potency as a manipulator of the subconscious by accident. The results did not appear on any report, because the tests were not performed in the lab at all.

He had given the drug to his children.

Both of his boys' symptoms were growing increasingly severe. At points in virtually every day, they had become almost uncontrollable, and the standard treatments had proved only marginally effective. The situation had grown so serious that both boys were assigned to a special school, which effectively meant they were relegated to a lower strata for life.

But Larry Kroom knew they were intelligent and good-hearted. It was all there in his journals, Rachel told her.

Kroom's agonizing, the love he felt for his boys, the helpless frustration. The lab results and animal testing had shown remarkable potential. To wait another two or three years until the clinical trials were completed would mean the drug would come online too late to have any impact on his children's crucial teenage years.

So he did what many other parents would have done. He stole samples from the lab.

Larry Kroom started with the boy who was older by eight minutes, because he was the worst off and was showing alarming signs of growing violent. Most ADHD patients leveled off at the approach to puberty, but in his son's case the symptoms were becoming increasingly severe, as though the only emotion he could freely express was rage. So he became SuenaMind's first human test subject.

The change was overnight.

Within seventy-two hours, the boy was laughing again. And not in the manic rage-filled manner that had marked his former outbursts. The boy's laugh was almost musical. In a week, he discovered the joy of reading. The scientist's personal journals recounted the astonishment and joy both parents felt, emotions that had been absent from their home for what seemed like years.

Three months later, Larry Kroom administered the drug to his younger son. Again the change was drastic and immediate.

Then, two weeks later, Kroom noticed a different change. One that was far less welcome. And extremely worrying.

The younger boy lost his ability to filter suggestion from reality. The older son read the younger boy a story at bedtime, and the next morning the child treated the story as part of his reality, part of his overall worldview.

Larry Kroom was a trained psychologist as well as biomedical scientist. He knew the patterns of hypnotic abuse, when ideas were force-instilled into the patients. The risk of manipulating a patient's subconscious was one reason so many clinicians refused to practice hypnosis at all. In normal cases, any patient over the age of four or five had a subconscious strong enough to filter out what was genuinely false, or in opposition to the patient's concept of self. Yet with some weaker patients, particularly those suffering from psychoses or showing evidence of schizoid tendencies, the risk was that any hypnotic suggestion would be adopted as truth.

Larry Kroom's journals described in exact detail how his younger boy lost the ability to tell the difference between inserted truth—including stories told to him or seen in movies and television shows—from reality. Once he had the opportunity to sleep, and to dream, the boy woke up assuming the fiction was fact.

At first Kroom had suspected it was a side effect of the new drug. And so he took two weeks off of work, to remain with his son through the period that the initial dose remained active, so as to buffer the child from any such further psychic insertions. But his older boy continued to show astonishing progress. And his younger son's behavior also improved. It was as though the drug was working, *despite* the side effect. And as was the case with most identical twins, the boys' bloodwork was almost identical. Which led Kroom to wonder if perhaps the problem lay not with SuenaMind, but with the *combination* of his new drug with something else.

There were basically two different patterns to ADHD treatment in young patients. The two boys had alternated between them. A number of children showed best results by moving from one to the other, and side effects were minimized. At the point when Kroom had administered the new drug, the older boy was going off one medicine, while the other had already started on the second.

Kroom took his younger boy off the other drug.

The result was a total and immediate cessation of all side effects.

The two boys never looked back.

At this point, Rachel began weeping so hard she could no longer breathe, much less speak. When she finally regained control, she said, "Kroom took his findings to the company's managing director. I checked. That man is now president of one of the banks involved in the One World scam."

Elena found herself glad that one of them was capable of shedding tears. "Rachel, I hope you're listening, because what I want to say to you is very important. Do you hear me?"

"Yes."

"I'm so sorry. I apologize with all my heart." Elena felt the band of sorrowful tension unwind from around her heart. "I distrusted you. I was wrong."

The words helped restore Rachel to a semblance of calm. "My career is a sham. Trevor Tenning has duped me from the first day I entered the building."

"SuenaMind is still a major breakthrough. The lab results and the help it gives children are all real. The side effect can be controlled. Your work is vital. None of this has been changed."

"But they *used* me."

"They used us both. Right now, I need you to *focus*. Can you do that?"

Rachel took a long breath. "Yes."

"Good. Now I want you to call Reed Thompson and tell him everything you told me. He's a friend and our ally in all this." Elena read off Reed's number. "Will you do that?"

Each moment drew Rachel further from the brink. "Yes. All right."

"Good. Then I want you to gather up all those journals and go somewhere safe. Call when you arrive. Don't phone me. My cell isn't safe. Ask Reed for a number you can use. Does anyone at SuenaMed know where you are?"

"Only my assistant, Reginald. I phoned him before I called you. I can't go in today, I—"

Alarms of electric clarity went off in her head. "Rachel, gather the journals and get out of there *now!*"

29

Elena tried to reach Reed, first on his cell and then at home. When the voice mail answered on both, she called his office and let it ring a dozen times and more. She then tried the university operator, who was clearly coming to the end of a very long shift. "Ma'am, nobody is ever in those offices this early on a Saturday."

"I've tried his home, he's not there."

The operator stifled a yawn. "He must be on his way in."

"Listen, you've got to help. This is an emergency."

"Hold on, then. I'll put you through to security."

"No, that's not—" But the operator was already gone. Elena paced to the closet and put back the clothes she had laid out for the day. When the security's voice mail came on, she cut the connection. Elena checked the bedside clock, which read ten minutes to eight. Jacob should be arriving at any minute. She tried his phone, and was switched immediately to voice mail. She ended the call and threw the phone at her pillow.

Elena opened her bedroom door far enough to tell Dorothy, "I've got to forget the workout and head straight to the university."

"Thought so. Personally, I never answer the phone in the morning, not until I'm ready to let the day in."

Elena dressed in a blouse of light gray silk and a slate-gray gabardine skirt. And pearls. She had decided on the ensemble while still on the phone with Rachel. This day would require all the solemn authority Elena could muster.

Or so she thought.

She was buttoning up her cuffs when there was a knock on her door. Dorothy set down her mug, walked over, and checked through the front door's spyhole. She turned to smile at Elena. "Looks like the beau who's not your beau got here early." She unlocked the door and said, "Always did like a man who knows how to be on time."

Dorothy was caught by the door crashing back. She was slammed against the wall with such force it overturned the vase on Elena's side table.

They had obviously planned their entry to the max. This much was clear in Elena's first milliseconds of shock and fear and dismay. They powered in together, their movements precise and deadly.

The taller of the two bodyguards held Jacob as a human shield. Jacob's eyes were the only part that moved of their own volition. He watched Elena with a look of visceral terror, fathomless and bleak.

The man directly behind the puppet master was a fireplug. Elena recognized him as the bodyguard who had cleared away the reporters as she had entered SuenaMed's headquarters. He aimed around Jacob and his mate, and shot Dorothy with a Taser.

A hallway connected the kitchen and the bedroom and the living-dining room to the front door. The foyer held a narrow side table and a chair. From the doorway it was possible to look down the hall, past the kitchen entry and through the living-

tight in her face, while they fastened Jacob to a third chair. Reginald made no attempt to hide his pleasure at having her under his control.

"The bonds on my wrists are too tight," Elena complained.

"Tough."

"My hands hurt."

"Not for long." He glanced over. "You about done?"

There was the sound of another plastic tie ratcheting shut. "That's it."

"Bring in the gear." He turned back to Elena. "You couldn't just take the payoff and enjoy yourself like any sane person. No. You had to make waves. You had to keep asking questions."

The fireplug opened the front door and brought in two black canvas grips. Reginald pointed at the floor to his right, where Elena could see what was happening, and went on, "Curiosity will soon kill the psychologist. Both of them. Pity."

"We know everything," Elena said.

"I'm sure you think you do." He waved at the docile bodies positioned to either side of her. "We've given your friend Jacob a sedative spray. It's another of the new products in the pipeline, all tied to what we're going to do with SuenaMind. This baby is a game changer. But you already know that, don't you?"

Reginald accepted a pair of surgical gloves from the bodyguard. He fitted them on and slipped an atomizer spray from his pocket. "Where was I going with this?"

The fireplug shrugged. "SuenaMind?"

"The sedative. Right. Give the cop a dose." As the guard pulled an atomizer from his pocket and sprayed Dorothy's face, Reginald went on, "One whiff of this new stuff and the patient is pliable as plastic. Got quite a kick, so I'm told. Makes the toughest go all happy-sappy. But once the dose is over, they don't remember a thing. Based on those new anesthetics doctors use for in-office procedures." He held up a second atomizer. "Then we give them the SuenaMind and the other ADHD drug together in a second spray. After that, and we're good to go."

Elena sought desperately for something, anything that might keep him talking. There was no real hope of a rescue. But anything was better than the doom she could see there in his gaze. "The attack in Miami. It was just a ruse."

"Of course it was. You needed to feel vulnerable. You needed to have an impetus to trust us."

"What about the market downturn? The bank's own stocks were hit worst of all."

"You're not thinking, Dr. Burroughs. It doesn't matter which way the market moves, if you know in advance."

"The insiders bet against their own companies."

"We all did. And made a fortune."

"And you murdered innocent people."

"Of course we did, Dr. Burroughs." He said to the others, "Give me a mask and back off."

The bodyguards retreated across the room. Reginald fitted a surgical mask around his mouth and nose, then sprayed the atomizer directly into the nostrils of first Dorothy and then Jacob. "We'll give that five minutes to reach the brain."

He stripped off the mask so he could leer at her. "Full effect starts wearing off after about six days. To have you do what we want, you'll need another taste. You know what it is we want, don't you, Dr. Burroughs? We want you to stop breathing."

Despite her terror, Elena managed, "The dreamer and the dead bankers. They had seizures because they threatened your plans."

"Just like you, Dr. Burroughs." Reginald had a truly terrible smile. "We order you to stop breathing. But your body fights the order as hard as it possibly can. Until it can't fight anymore."

He fitted on a surgical mask, then dug in the canvas carryall and came up with a black face mask like a diver would wear. A flexible black hose dangled from the base, where it connected to a shiny metal canister. "We designed this apparatus to deal with what you might call the hostile patient."

She hated herself for begging. But she couldn't stop the words from emerging through her clenched teeth. "Don't. Please."

"You're about to discover we've refined the process considerably. We can instruct the patient to dream anything, then wake up and do anything."

"Let them go."

"No problem. Dorothy here will drive home and have an accident with her gun, won't you, dear? And Jacob, he'll fly back to Atlanta and pick up his car from the airport and unfortunately swerve off the road. He won't survive, I'm sorry to say. Best get your farewells over while there's still time."

"No, don't—"

"Oh, and I've got something very special in store for Reed Thompson. And the girl. What's her name?" He reached with the mask toward her. Despite Elena's thrashing about, he fitted the mask over her face and lashed it into place. He saved his worst smile for last. "Oh, now I remember. Stacy. Sweet dreams, Dr. Burroughs."

31

Elena watched it all unfold from an impossible distance, helpless to defend herself, unable to bring things into real focus. She drank in the words Reginald spoke as she would a poison. She had no choice. Her will was gone.

She heard the canister hiss into the mask. She held her breath as long as she could, and struggled until it felt like her wrists were lacerated. None of it mattered. Reginald kept his face in tight enough to observe her through the Plexiglas. His expression was almost clinical, like a scientist preparing to dissect an insect. When she had gasped through a trio of sobbing breaths, he stripped off the mask, then moved over and sprayed first Dorothy and then Jacob with the SuenaMind mixture. He spoke to them with precise calm, glancing at Elena from time to time, making sure she was listening. Which of course, she was. She had no choice.

He returned and squatted down in front of her chair. When he smiled, a veil rippled across Elena's vision. It was as close to a response as she could come.

"I've saved the best for last." Reginald gave her the orders with a sense of genuine satisfaction. "When you come out of this, everything that's happened here will be just another bad dream. But you'll feel like you're coming down with a cold. No, call it the flu. You'll phone in sick, then lay down for a nap."

He rose from his position in front of her chair, smiled down at her, and finished, "And you know what happens when bad girls fall asleep, don't you?"

She felt trapped in layers of invisible chains, held far beneath the surface. Even so, Reginald's leer rippled and ran momentarily, as her frustrated rage fought for air.

"No," Elena moaned.

All three men turned to her. "You hear that?" Reginald asked.

The tall one said, "I thought they couldn't speak."

"It's nothing. She moaned," Reginald said. He leaned in closer still. "You will fall asleep, and you will stop breathing. Permanently."

Elena struggled and fought, and managed, "Don't."

The three exchanged a glance. "Lady's got some chops," the fireplug said.

"Cut her loose," Reginald ordered.

Even after they released her, they continued to hold her captive. A tiny segment of her mind knew this, and saw what was happening, and wept.

Reginald walked behind her chair and said, "Stand up." He then guided her to her feet by gripping her upper arms and steadying her as she rose. When he was certain she could manage on her own, he said, "Go make coffee."

The small hidden component of herself observed as she turned and shuffled into the kitchen. Behind her, Reginald said, "See how easy it is to make the lady behave?"

Again the faint ripple passed over her eyes, another veil of rage, there and gone. She watched her hands fumble through the

process of filling the glass pot with water. Her hands were unsteady, and she spilled water on the counter as she filled the
brewer's reservoir. She had even more trouble with the coffee,
dumping as much on the counter as she did in the basket. She fit
the pot on the eye and turned on the machine. Then she stood
there, waiting. Reginald checked on her when the machine
started gurgling. "Clean up this mess."

She took the towel from its place on the oven handle and did
as she was told. Then she went back to standing in front of the
machine. The cabinet directly in front of her was covered with a
walnut veneer. One tiny strip of the veneer had frayed by the
brass knob, where years of use had gradually taken its toll. The
pressed plywood underneath was revealed, not much, smaller
than the nail on her little finger. Elena had never noticed it
before. She did not really notice it now. She stood there because
she was incapable of moving without another direct order.

Reginald called, "Come in here, Dr. Burroughs. I want you
to see something."

She left the kitchen and shuffled back into the living room,
where Reginald directed her into a chair stationed in front of the
television. Dorothy and Jacob remained seated in their chairs,
facing the foyer wall, staring at nothing.

"No, don't look at them, Dr. Burroughs. Watch the screen.
Pay careful attention."

On the news channel, Trevor Tenning stood before a battery
of microphones. Elena's vision rippled once more, as another
surge of rage almost managed to cross the impossible distance
and break free.

SuenaMed's CEO was both direct and diplomatic. His demeanor invited calm, confidence, even affection. He said, "Our
attitude toward 'too big to fail' is outdated. The current crisis has
pushed the world beyond all that. If we are going to salvage our
economic future, we must accept this as fact and go in a new di-

rection. We need to create a world banking system, a system of universal financial governance. One so large and powerful it can *never* fail."

One of the journalists called up, "Doesn't this threaten the rights and freedoms of individuals and nations?"

"Of course it does. But isn't this also precisely what has happened with this present crisis? Who is free of these horrible effects? Which nation, which family? Isn't it worth giving up some fragment of our freedom in order to make a clear and safe tomorrow? The One World Bank consortium *guarantees* financial stability. So the nations lose the right to choose a course that leads to disaster. So what? The current system is a *failure*. If we want to survive, if we want to enter a new era of growth and strength, we have no choice but change."

Reginald cut off the television. He squatted in front of her, so close his face filled her immobile gaze. "You see why your investigation was so futile, Dr. Burroughs? You and your puny band could never stop this juggernaut. Never. Sharper minds than yours have worked and planned for years." He poked her shoulder. "Minds like my own, Dr. Burroughs. After bowing and scraping to Rachel Lamprey for months, what difference does it make, cleaning up a few loose ends? Nothing, that's what. I look forward to taking care of her next."

A bodyguard called from the kitchen, "What do I do with this coffee?"

"Give them half a mug each." Reginald straightened, but stood where he could loom over her. "Order them to take the mug and sip it slowly. Talk to them like you would a child."

"Then what?"

"Those two will start coming out in about ten minutes. They'll leave here, follow their instructions, and poof. Our problem is over. This one will take a little longer. We need to be gone by then." He leaned over once more. "Which is a pity. It really is.

I'd love to stay for the whole show. But we can't stay, can we? Not when we've never been here."

The taller bodyguard brought Reginald a mug. "They won't remember us?"

"You heard what I told them. We're nothing. A bad dream." He gestured to Elena. "Give her the mug."

The taller bodyguard waved a hand before her eyes. "What happens if I slap her hard?"

"Don't."

"No, I mean, will it wake her up?"

"I know what you meant, and I'm telling you not to do it." Reginald took the coffee from him and said, "Go pack our gear." He handed her the mug and said, "Drink it slowly. It's hot."

She did as she was told, blowing and sipping. She felt the liquid course down her throat. She knew at some deep level that she only had a few minutes left. Because as soon as she woke up, she was going to call the university, claim illness, then treat her wrists and lie down and take a nap.

And she would never wake up again.

But she could do nothing. Not even weep for her own demise.

"Check around carefully. Take any valuables you can find; make it look like a burglary." Reginald looked at her. "Okay. Finish your coffee. It's almost time to—"

The door exploded inward, followed by a rush of so many bodies they could not be counted. The sound was massive. *"Stop! Police! Hands where we can see them! Down! Everybody down!"*

Elena jerked as though electrocuted. She did not merely draw the world back into clarity. Her awareness *surged* back. She *exploded* back to a state of full alert.

Even so, her body remained trapped and sluggish.

She forced her head to turn to the left. It required a very conscious effort, giving herself precise instructions over and over. Turn and keep turning.

She saw two different kinds of uniforms. She realized some of the people were university security. Which could mean only one thing.

A surge of emotion rose within her, a relief so strong she could not stop the tears. *"Reed!"*

"Here, Elena. I'm here."

She tried to blink away the tears, but they kept coming so fast she could not clear her vision. Reed was a shadowy blur in front of her, kneeling so as to cradle her face in his hands. But his voice was intense and caring and crystal clear. "My darling, what have they done to you?"

She made both her hands come up to grip his arms. Her speech felt slurred, but even so it carried all the desperate need she could muster. *"Tell me not to dream."*

32

They were rushed to the regional hospital. Elena and the others were placed in the ICU under strict observation. A police officer remained stationed outside her alcove. Bob Meadows was flown up from Miami, and he hypnotized all three of them, Elena and Dorothy and Jacob. When she emerged from the treatment, she found Bob very pale, very troubled. She had to smile at that. It was so good to let someone else worry for her just then.

And worry they did. Elena was almost never alone. Only one visitor at a time was permitted in the ICU, which meant she had a steady solitary stream. Bob Meadows was replaced by Reed, then Stacy, then Rachel, then Stacy again. The young girl refused to go to school. She took all of her meals at Elena's bedside. The only time she willingly gave up her chair was when her father appeared.

Elena's dreams were horrid. Given the sounds emanating from the alcoves to either side of her own, Elena assumed the others experienced similar troubles while asleep. She did not have nightmares so much as vague whispers. They attacked and clawed at her, trying to drag her back into a dark hole that loomed just beyond her horizon.

On the second day the hospital staff shifted them to private rooms on the third floor. Elena insisted upon seeing the others. Dorothy spent most of their time together apologizing, as though she had let Elena down. Elena left only when she was certain the woman understood Elena felt nothing but gratitude.

Jacob remained hollowed and gouged by his ordeal. Elena sat in the chair next to his bed, holding his hand, while a nurse and Bob Meadows hovered by the door. He confessed, "I feel so weak."

"I know. So do I. Bob says it's the result of fighting off the subconscious commands."

"Just like a patient recovering from a bad psychosis or nervous attack," Bob confirmed. "Nervous energy depletion has as strong an impact on the system as physical exertion."

Jacob clutched at her with his gaze. "I'm scared."

She nodded. "I know."

"And my dreams." His swallow was audible. "Will they stop?"

"With time," Bob assured them both. "Gradually."

Jacob's gaze never left Elena. "It all happened, didn't it? They came and they dosed me and they told me to . . ."

Elena held his hand and endured her own recollections. Part of Bob's therapy required them to recall everything, and thus bring their conscious mind into the process of throwing off the induced commands.

"Elena."

"I'm here."

"The night before. When we were in the car."

She nodded. "We prayed together."

Bob's intake of breath was audible across the room. Jacob glanced at his friend for the first time since Elena had seated herself. Jacob turned back to her and said, "Do you think it would help to pray now?"

She smiled for the first time in what felt like years. "I think it would help us both." She reached out to where Bob was already approaching. "Let's bow our heads."

33

⬥────────────⬥

The president's house had a small apartment over the three-car garage. The apartment consisted of a living-dining-kitchen area and a small bedroom and a bathroom. The bedroom held a queen-size bed, with scarcely enough room left over for one occupant to slip around sideways. The closet was two feet square. The shower was almost as small as the closet. The rooms were under the eaves, and the ceiling sloped so that an adult could not stand up by the outer walls.

Elena thought it was perfect. It had all the comforting closeness of a cocoon. What was more, staying here meant she did not need to be alone. Or confront the memories waiting back in her condo.

She knew she would need to go back. Recall everything. Work through it all bit by bit. This was the framework upon which mental health was built. Face the bad things squarely. Work through them honestly. And move on. Elena knew this was coming.

Just not yet.

She did not even return for her clothes. Reed and Stacy saw the dread in her eyes as they pulled into her parking area, and volunteered to go inside for her. Elena stayed in the car, staring out over the sparkling waters, listening to the wind whistle past the car. The hurricane was apparently staying off the coast. The latest tracking models showed it not touching land. Yet even the storm's outer trail was enough to buffet the car. They were expecting heavy rains that evening. But as she waited for father and daughter to return, the sun was brilliant and the AC kept the car cool. Elena kept her gaze fastened on the river and the pelicans diving for fish, and willed herself not to look at the door to her home, or give in to the memories that lurked beyond the edges of her vision.

That night they all gathered for a final dinner. Jacob was flying back to Atlanta the next day. Bob Meadows was going with him, to offer friendship and comfort and to help with patients that Jacob was not yet ready to meet. Dorothy's daughter had arrived from Minneapolis and remained close to her mother's side. Rachel Lamprey was silent and regal and shaken to her core, and ate almost nothing. They filled the formal dining room. Reed and Stacy served, refusing all offers of help. Elena sat facing the portrait of Stacy's mother. Her eyes were repeatedly drawn back to the painting. She hoped the woman's smile was meant at least in part to welcome her.

After dinner they gathered in the parlor and watched the news coverage of a severely chastened Trevor Tenning being led into custody. This was followed by a press conference held by Mario Suarez, who now served as head of the Senate Banking and Finance Committee.

For once, the senator met the gathered press without his customary rage. "The crisis masterminded by out-of-control banks has been diverted. Our task is to ensure these institutions never again are in a position to overthrow the democratic process."

As the interview wound down, Reed said, "I spoke with Agatha this afternoon. They'll be going after convictions, but slowly. The first goal is to stabilize the markets and assure there will be no destructive repercussions. The last thing we want is a financial meltdown."

They closed the evening with prayer. Rachel did not speak, but neither did she draw back when the people to either side reached for her hands. Twice Elena opened her eyes to find the woman's dark gaze glittering in the room's comforting glow, staring at something only she could see.

The evening farewells lingered quite a while. Outside the open doorway, the first squall rushed through, lashing the pavement with wind and rain. Jacob held Elena long enough for the sleeves of her dress to become damp. "Will I ever stop being afraid?"

"Soon," she replied, hoping it would be true for them both. "You know you can call me anytime. Day or night."

Bob Meadows waited until Jacob had run to the car before saying, "You'll probably need therapy to work through all this."

"I am well aware of this, Bob."

"I'm just saying, I'd consider it an honor to help out. I have several long-distance patients. Sessions via videoconference work well enough in their cases."

She embraced him a second time. "You're a good friend."

Rachel Lamprey was the last to depart. She stood behind the others, well inside the front foyer. Her dark eyes were trapped within deep hollows, as though she had not slept at all since the night she had spent searching the former lab director's basement. She stared at the rain and the night with abject defeat.

Elena asked Reed to shut the door and took Rachel by the arm. She guided the SuenaMed executive over to a bench by the wall. It was antique oak and not very comfortable, something intended as a decorative item. Elena did not mind. She did not think Rachel even noticed.

Elena said, "I want you to think about something."

Rachel did not speak. Her gaze remained held by whatever she saw beyond the closed door.

"This is very important."

Rachel's eyes gradually tracked over. "Can you ever forgive me?"

"For what? You did only what you thought was right. And best. For your company, for us, and for the world."

"And I got everything wrong."

"We all did. We let them use us. Me, you, a United States senator, leaders from around the globe. They duped us. It was a brilliant scam. And they almost pulled it off."

"Because of me."

"No, Rachel." Despite two days of almost continuous rest, Elena still had very little energy. But she put as much as she could into saying, "If it weren't for you, they would have won."

Rachel blinked slowly. Elena saw the words register. She went on, "And your company still needs you."

This pushed her back hard against the wall. "What?"

"Think about it. SuenaMind is still a huge discovery."

"You can't be serious. What about the side effects?"

"Remember what you found in the scientist's notes? Suena-Mind by itself is utterly safe. It is only when taken with another drug that it has this impact on the dream state. You and I both know doctors can be advised to monitor patients and additives can be inserted to negate these joint effects."

"But . . ." She tasted several responses. "I'm not sure I'm ready for this. Or ever will be."

"What if I were to help you?"

She looked at Elena then. Really looked. "You would do this? Come to work with us?"

"As a consultant. Absolutely. Think about it. We have a drug that, when combined with other substances, actually has the power to influence the most basic components of the human psyche. This isn't simply going to vanish because of one group's attempt to manipulate human events. We have to study this, channel it, and determine how it can be used for good. I can name you half a dozen clinical issues, where there is currently no treatment at all, that could potentially be resolved with this compound."

"I—I'll think about it."

"Good. Let's talk tomorrow." She steadied Rachel as she rose to her feet. "Promise me you'll try to get some rest."

She walked with Rachel to where Reed held the door open. As they embraced, Elena whispered, "Miriam would be very proud of you."

34

⸙━━━━━━━⸙

Her good-nights with Reed and Stacy were as warm as they were easy. There was more than closeness between them. It was as if they had already decided to make Elena a permanent part of their home and their lives. While she appreciated the sentiment more than she could say, Elena knew she was going to have to relocate the next day. Nice as it was, she could not afford to let Reed become the brunt of unfounded rumor.

Especially since she hoped one day to move back in here. Permanently.

Elena remained downstairs in the kitchen and listened to them move about upstairs, preparing for bed. She was tired in the manner of needing far more than one night's rest. A solitary light burned over the stove, casting the room in a soft glow. She was seated at the table by the bay windows, her back to the storm, looking over a kitchen that she hoped would one day be her own. Beyond the light's reach was the doorway leading to the front rooms, where another woman stood in regal solitude, overseeing her former domain. Elena offered a swift prayer that she would be found worthy of helping to raise that precious child, and share love with this good man.

Her eyelids were growing heavy, but there was one more thing that needed doing to make the day complete. She picked up her cell phone and hit redial by the one number that had called her every day since the adventure had begun.

Elena greeted Vicki Ferrell, her New York editor, with "I hope I'm not calling too late."

"Girl, I've been waiting for this call with bated breath. What kind of author and friend leaves her editor dangling like this?"

"I've been a little busy."

"When you stopped showing up for the conferences, I panicked. Then when this thing started blowing up, I panicked some more." Vicki Ferrell paused, then asked, "How are you, really?"

"Really, I'm good and getting better."

"What happened down there, girl?"

"That's why I'm calling." Elena stared out beyond the kitchen and the haven of this home, out past the night and the storm. She looked beyond even tomorrow, out to a day where she could walk with ease and breathe freely and know her nightmares were well and truly behind her. Bob Meadows was right. Given everything she had experienced, the only way this could happen would be through some form of therapy. Laying it all out, in utter honesty, and examining it through the lenses of truth and prayer.

"Elena, are you still there?"

"I'm here." She took a long breath. "I'm ready to write my new book."

A NOTE FROM THE AUTHOR

The research that went into the making of this book covers almost my entire adult life. Strands from many different segments of my past have become woven together in these pages.

My undergraduate studies took place at Wake Forest University in North Carolina, my home state. I earned a BA in two entirely different fields: economics and psychology. Following this, I traveled to London, where I studied for a Master of Science in international finance. There I continued to feed my fascination about the human mind, by doing further studies in industrial psychology.

Following a year when I lectured at a Swiss university, I was hired by a pharmaceutical company. They specialized in what are known as generics, or drugs that have lost their patent protection and thus can be made by anyone. It is a highly competitive field, and I loved the work. We were one of the largest suppliers of antibiotics to Africa and the Middle East, and I traveled more than I stayed at home. Eventually I was promoted to the position of marketing manager. I stayed with them for four years.

I then accepted a position as director of the European operations of a business advisory group. We were based in Düsseldorf, Germany, and operated in eleven countries. In my second year, I came to faith. Two weeks later, I began writing. I can still remember the almost ferocious intensity of that moment, when I genuinely heard the call of God. It is with such humble gratitude that I sit here now, twenty years later, and look back at the incredible path my life has taken since that day. It was far from easy or straightforward—I wrote for nine years and completed seven novels before my first was accepted for publication. But the sense of selfless joy I discovered in those early days has only intensified over the years.

If readers are interested in more details about how I came to be where I am, and what went into the formation of this book, they are invited to visit my website at www.DavisBunn.com.

READING GROUP GUIDE

Introduction

Just when the world's foremost expert on dream analysis, Dr. Elena Burroughs, thinks she is getting her life back under control after losing her position at Oxford University and the man she hoped to fall in love with, she is approached by Rachel Lamprey, the product manager of an innovative new ADHD treatment about to hit the market. Rachel asks for Elena's help with a clinical trial participant who has had a disturbing dream foretelling a cataclysmic global financial collapse. But even more alarming is the fact that fifteen people scattered across the globe—including Elena herself—begin to experience the same repetitive, devastating dreams of economic ruin just as one bank crisis follows another, suggesting that these aren't merely dreams.

As Elena searches for answers in her professional networks, she is forced to form an unlikely alliance with one of her most vehement critics and is drawn back into the spotlight as the public face of the so-called dreamers. Elena and her collaborators must race against the clock to find the connection between the dreams and the very real events threatening a financial melt-down. It's no longer about just dreams: it's about survival.

Topics & Questions
for Discussion

1. Would you help a woman like Rachel when she first comes to Elena for help with her test subject? What questions would you ask her before proceeding? Do you trust her?

2. What kind of role did the Florida landscape play in the novel? How does the weather reflect the turmoil the characters are experiencing?

3. How would you react if you experienced one of these terrible dreams? How would you react when you found out that others had the exact same dream?

4. How does Reed serve as a spiritual guide for Elena? Do you think she needs his guidance?

5. Elena is drawn into the public eye in Davis Bunn's novel, *Book of Dreams,* and is forced back into the spotlight in this sequel, *Hidden in Dreams.* Have you ever been forced or called to do something against your own intuition or choice? What did you do?

6. While Jacob's faith journey is just beginning, his skepticism starts to fade as even he can no longer deny the existence of a guiding force in the world. What do you think changes him?

7. Writing is said to be the "cheapest form of therapy." Is Elena right to agree to write a second book about her experiences?

8. How do the fears of a global financial crisis resonate with current headlines and your own personal experiences? Did any of the scenes or descriptions in *Hidden in Dreams* particularly resonate with you?

9. Have you ever had a dream that significantly affected you? Do you typically remember your dreams?

10. Which character did you connect with most? Which character do you share the most similar behaviors or traits with?

11. Elena and Stacy form a pseudo mother-daughter relationship. How does their relationship evolve? Do you think Elena is a good role model for Stacy? Is Stacy a role model herself for Elena?

12. Elena says, "At its best, religion is a matter of creating an earthly structure in which to express the wonder of connecting with the divine. At its worst, religion seeks to fit God into a safe and comfortable little box" (p. 111). Do you agree with Elena's statement? Why or why not? Do any other characters offer a different perspective on religion in the novel?

Enhance Your Book Club

1. Experiment with keeping a dream journal. Keep your journal next to your bed and record your dreams as soon as you wake up each morning. Dreams fade quickly, so it is important to write them down soon after you awaken! Look for interesting patterns or themes as you record more dreams and share them with your book club members. For help with decoding your dreams, visit www.DreamMoods.com or www.TheCuriousDreamer.com.

2. If you haven't already, go back to the start of Elena Burroughs's journey in the public eye by reading *Book of Dreams*, the prequel to *Hidden in Dreams*. Discuss the differences between the two books and how Elena has grown as a character.

3. Find out more about the author by visiting www.DavisBunn .com. Discover more about Davis's upcoming projects and discuss with other readers in the web forums. If you submit a review of *Hidden in Dreams*, it might be chosen to be shared on Davis's blog!

Also available from

DAVIS
BUNN

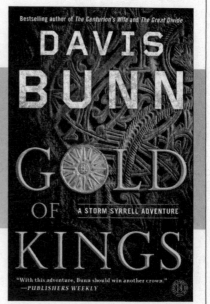